THE MYSTERY OFF
OLD TELEGRAPH ROAD

Trixie Belden

Your TRIXIE BELDEN Library

Trixie Belden and the MYSTERY OFF OLD TELEGRAPH ROAD

BY KATHRYN KENNY

Cover by Jack Wacker

GOLDEN PRESS
Western Publishing Company, Inc.
Racine, Wisconsin

CONTENTS

THE MYSTERY OFF
OLD TELEGRAPH ROAD

The Art Fair • 1

PLEASE HURRY, TRIXIE," Honey Wheeler urged her best friend. "I want to have as much time as possible at the art fair, and Ben said he'd only wait half an hour to give us a ride home."

Trixie Belden put her books in her locker and slammed the door a little harder than was necessary. As she followed Honey to the gymnasium, where the art fair was being held, she thought about how much things had changed since Honey's cousin Ben Riker had been staying with the Wheeler family.

Honey Wheeler had been Trixie's best friend since the day the Wheeler family moved into the

Manor House, the big mansion on the hill just west of Crabapple Farm where Trixie lived with her parents and her three brothers. Together, Honey and Trixie had solved several mysteries, and they planned to open the Belden-Wheeler Detective Agency after they finished school.

One of their first cases had been to find Jim Frayne, who had run away to upstate New York to get away from his cruel stepfather. Honey's parents had adopted Jim, and Honey, Jim, and Trixie, together with Trixie's two older brothers, Mart and Brian, had formed a club called the Bob-Whites of the Glen. Two other members, Dan Mangan and Di Lynch, had been added to the club since then. The Bob-Whites devoted themselves to helping others and to having fun, as well as to solving the mysteries in which Trixie was constantly getting them involved.

But that's all changed now, Trixie thought grudgingly. *Ever since Ben Riker arrived last month, Honey and Jim have been so busy trying to keep him out of trouble that there hasn't been time for anything else. I don't know how Honey can stand him.*

Honey's cousin Ben had always been a show-off and a practical joker, plaguing the family with pranks like filling the sugar bowl with salt. But his jokes had been harmless enough until a few

14

months before, when he had fallen in with a bad group at the expensive boarding school he'd been attending. With his grades slipping and his behavior getting him closer and closer to real trouble, he had been sent to stay with the Wheelers for a while, in hopes that Jim and Honey—and the Beldens, too—would be a good influence.

It certainly hasn't worked that way so far, Trixie reflected as she and Honey entered the gym. *All he's done since he came to Sleepyside is to get in with a crowd that's as bad as the one at his boarding school. And even though Honey and Jim try to be nice to him and plan things to do together, he always seems bored and ungrateful when he's around them.*

"I know what you're thinking, Trixie," Honey said, interrupting Trixie's troubled thoughts. "It is too bad that we have only half an hour to spend at the art fair. I know that Jim or Brian would have given us all the time we wanted. They might even have come along with us if they weren't busy with other things. But with Ben— Well, at least he did agree to give us a ride home. Sometimes I think Ben really would like to be helpful and to get along better with the rest of us, but he's afraid to show it."

"Why would someone be afraid to show that he's a nice person?" Trixie asked. "That doesn't make any sense at all to me."

"That's because you've never had to go to one of those dreadful boarding schools, Trixie," Honey told her. "Believe me, I know. You get so lonely, away from your family all the time except for holidays, that feeling that you belong to a group becomes dreadfully important. You don't want to do anything that will make your group lose respect for you. And in Ben's case, the group he belongs to thinks it's cool to get into mischief and not to care about schoolwork or helping other people. So Ben goes along with the crowd. I know it's hard for you to understand, because you've always had loving parents and two older brothers to encourage you to do the right thing. But everyone isn't as lucky as you've been, Trixie."

Honey's huge hazel eyes clouded over, and she lowered her head so that her shoulder-length honey-blond hair would shade her face for a moment. Trixie knew that her friend was thinking about the days before she'd come to live in Sleepyside, when she, too, had been sent away to boarding schools in the winter and to camps during the summer and had come to think that her parents didn't care about her. All that had changed for Honey when her parents bought the Manor House and hired Miss Trask, Honey's former math teacher, to look after Honey while they were on their frequent travels. But Trixie knew that the memories of the earlier times were still painful for her friend.

"I'm sorry, Honey," Trixie said. "You're right about my not understanding. I guess I'm spoiled by all the affection I've always got from my family. I'll try to be more patient with Ben."

Honey raised her head and smiled at Trixie. "You're wonderful to keep trying. I know he's *my* cousin, not yours. But I think he'll come around soon, and then you'll like him. Just wait and see."

I'll wait, Trixie thought, *but I don't think I'm going to see any big change—not in Ben Riker.*

Trixie was so lost in her thoughts about Ben Riker and the problems he'd caused that it took her a while to bring her attention back to the art fair. When she did, it was with a growing feeling of disappointment.

This art fair was the first ever to be held at Sleepyside Junior-Senior High School. Posters had been up in the school corridors for over a week announcing it, and Trixie and Honey had both been eager to go—Honey because she had an appreciation of beautiful things and Trixie because she was always curious about a new event, especially one that raised money for a worthy cause, like new equipment for the art department.

The girls had planned to stay after school this

Friday to attend the art fair, even though it would mean missing the school bus, and they were heartbroken when Dan, Jim, and Brian, the only Bob-Whites who had driver's licenses, had other plans and couldn't give them a ride home. In desperation, Honey had asked Ben, who had consented to wait half an hour, but no more. Both girls felt it was better than nothing, although Trixie harbored the thought that Ben couldn't have any plans that were so important that he couldn't have waited longer. But now that they were actually at the art fair. . . .

"It looks like half an hour will be plenty of time, doesn't it?" Trixie whispered to Honey.

"It certainly isn't what I'd expected," Honey said tactfully.

The gymnasium, which was always filled to overflowing at school carnival time, looked empty. There were only a few tables around the center of the gym and a few exhibits of paintings and drawings along the walls. Not very many students had shown an interest in attending the fair, and only one or two people stood in front of each exhibit.

"Well, as long as we're here, we might as well look around," Trixie said, walking to the nearest table. The table held a small collection of pottery cups and vases. Even to Trixie's untrained eye, they looked lopsided and amateurish. She felt vaguely embarrassed, not knowing what to say to Amy Morrisey, a girl she knew from her English class, who was standing behind the table. To her relief, Honey's tact once again came to the rescue.

"I've always been amazed that someone can take a lump of clay and put it on a wheel and turn that with their feet while they work the clay with their hands. It takes a lot more coordination than I'll ever have!" Honey told Amy.

Amy laughed. "Even with lots of coordination, it still takes a lot of practice. I've only been at it for two years, and with just one wheel in the art department, I haven't had as much practice as I need to be really good. But I'm a lot better than I was. You should have seen the first things I turned out. They looked like something a caveman might have done!"

"This must be one of your most recent things," Honey said, pointing to a large vase with a blue glaze. "It's really quite good."

"It's my favorite," Amy admitted. "I almost didn't put it in the show because I'd like to keep it. But I decided that was a selfish attitude. The art department needs the money so badly, and this is the only thing I've done that's good enough to ask a decent price for." She shrugged. "I finally told myself I can't really lose, either way. If it doesn't sell, I get to keep it. And if it does, I have the satisfaction of knowing that the money will go to the art department."

"That's terrific! I can never make myself think that way," Trixie said, wrinkling her freckled nose and shaking her head so that her sandy curls bounced. "No matter how good the cause is, I just hate to give up anything of my own for it."

"That's not true," Honey said loyally. "Why, Trixie is the most generous person I've ever known. She gets an allowance from her parents for doing housework and baby-sitting for her little brother, and even though she has to give up all that time, she's always willing to donate her money to—" Honey stopped herself from saying "to the club treasury" because the Bob-Whites were sworn not to tell that they all contributed their earnings to the treasury to be used for worthy causes. "To people who need it," Honey finished. "And once she gave a valuable diamond ring to Mr. Lytell, who owns a store out near us, so he'd hold the car her brother Brian wanted to buy." Honey saw her friend blushing at the praise and didn't continue her list of Trixie's unselfish acts.

Trixie's embarrassment was caused partly from hearing Honey telling Amy about her virtues, but it was also partly because she knew that she hadn't been very gracious about giving up the companionship of Honey and Jim to the worthy cause of trying to keep Ben Riker from getting into trouble. *I've just got to be more understanding about Ben,* she thought.

Aloud she said, "It was easy to give up that diamond because I'd never wear it, anyway, but to sell something I'd made— Well, I still think you're terrific to do it, and I hope everything works out for you."

Saying good-bye to Amy, Trixie and Honey moved on through the gym, looking at exhibits of watercolors, oil paintings, and stained glass. At nearly every exhibit, they heard the same complaint: The young artists knew that the works they were showing weren't very good, but the lack of supplies and equipment made it difficult to produce really first-rate things.

"I wish there were something we could do," Trixie told Honey after they'd made a discouraging round of most of the exhibits. "It seems so unfair that talented people should be held back because they don't have the supplies they need."

"I know," Honey agreed. "The art department obviously needs a lot more money, but I don't think they're going to raise much at this art fair. So few people are here, and nobody seems to be buying anything."

"Including us," Trixie said ruefully. "But I

21

haven't seen anything I really like. And I don't want to buy just anything. With the rules we Bob-Whites have about working for the money in our treasury, I've learned how important it is to be able to feel as though you've earned what you get, instead of taking charity."

"Exactly," Honey agreed. "I think that's been an even more important lesson for me than it has been for you, Trixie. We've had a lot of money ever since I can remember, and I used to just ask for whatever I wanted. But since I've been a Bob-White and earned money by doing mending for your mother and mine, I feel a lot better about myself. If we buy something here not because we like it but just because we want to donate money to the art department, the artist will know it, and that would hurt."

"Well, there are still a few things we haven't looked at," Trixie said. "Let's hurry and see the rest of the exhibits before our time is up. There might be some pleasant surprises."

Without waiting for a reply from Honey, Trixie started off across the gym. Suddenly she felt Honey grasp her arm and heard her friend gasp.

"Look, Trixie," Honey said. "It's the Manor House!"

A Shattered Vase • 2

TRIXIE FOLLOWED her friend's gaze to the far side of the gym, where a collection of pen-and-ink drawings was hanging against the wall.

"It *is* the Manor House!" Trixie exclaimed. "I can recognize it from clear over here. Oh, and, Honey, there's Crabapple Farm, too! Let's go!"

Trixie almost ran across the gym to the exhibit, while Honey followed at a more dignified pace.

Getting closer to the collection of drawings, Trixie saw several other places from the Sleepyside area that she recognized. "Look, Honey," she said. "There's Town Hall, and there's Hoppy." She leaned forward to peer at the signature on the drawing. " 'Nicholas William Roberts the third.' Is that you?" she asked, turning to a serious-looking, dark-haired boy standing nearby.

"I'm Nick Roberts," he told her. "But who's Hoppy?"

Trixie and Honey looked at each other and giggled. "That's what we call the grasshopper weather vane on top of the Town Hall building," Trixie explained. "My mother always thought, when she was a girl, that saying hello to Hoppy brought good luck. And she passed the tradition on to me. Oh, I'm Trixie Belden, by the way, and this is Honey Wheeler," Trixie added, remembering her manners.

"I read about you in the *Sleepyside Sun,*" Nick Roberts said. "You're the ones who solved the mystery about the disappearance of the grasshopper from the steeple of Town Hall. Then you donated the reward money to the city to get the weather vane replated. It's an honor to have such celebrities at our art fair," he added in a teasing tone.

While Trixie blushed, Honey said, "You're the one who should be a celebrity, Nick. These drawings are just marvelous. This is where I live." Honey pointed to the drawing of the Manor House. "And this house here, with all the big old crab-apple trees around it, is Trixie's. We recognized

24

them from across the gym, and we just had to come over here and see them up close."

"They're even better up close," Trixie added, forgetting her embarrassment as she inspected the drawing of Crabapple Farm. "Every detail is perfect. There are the windows of my room, with those crabapple branches almost touching them. I can even see Bobby's bike in the front yard. He 'forgotted' to put it away, as usual."

"The Manor House is perfect, too," Honey said. "There are Susie and Starlight in the paddock in front of the stable. How do you manage to do such beautiful drawings, Nick?"

"I have one here that I'm working on," Nick replied, "if you'd like a brief demonstration." When both girls nodded eagerly, Nick sat down at a table in front of his collection of drawings and showed them the picture he was working on.

"I work from a photograph," he told them. "That way I can work on the drawing for as long as I have to, whenever I have time, without being bothered by changes in light because of the time of day or the weather.

"I work on illustration board," he continued, "which is fairly heavy. It comes in a lot of textures and colors, so I can get different effects. The pen I use is called a technical pen, and it's really just a hollow metal tube with a cartridge full of ink

25

attached to it. The tubes come in several different sizes to give different widths of line. For example, I might use a size four for the outlines of the house, and then I'd switch to a smaller size, like a two- or three-aught, for fine lines like the twigs of the crabapple trees at Trixie's house. I've already done a pencil sketch of this photograph of the Glen Road Inn, and now I just trace over the pencil and fill in the details with the pen."

As Honey and Trixie watched, the Glen Road Inn began to take shape under Nick's rapidly moving hand. He filled in shadowy areas and gave some places depth with tiny crisscrossed lines, or "cross-hatching," as he called them.

"It must be wonderful to be so talented," Trixie said admiringly. "How did you get interested in pen-and-ink?"

Trixie saw the muscles in Nick's jaw tighten as he dropped the pen almost contemptuously onto the table. "Actually," he said, "I didn't choose pen-and-ink. It chose me." Seeing the girls' mystified looks, he explained, "The other media, like watercolors and oils, are just plain too expensive. A good brush can cost twenty dollars. And one tube of oil paint is around four dollars. Add the cost of canvas and cleaners and multiply that by the number of colors you'd need to do justice to a painting and—well, you get the idea."

"Gleeps!" Trixie exclaimed. "I'll say I do! Some of the other artists here have told us about the lack of money for art supplies and how it's been bothering them, but nobody put it quite as, uh, *vividly,* as you have. No wonder the art department decided to put on this art fair."

"That was my idea," Nick said. "You see, I want to go on to art school after I graduate, but no good school will take me on the basis of these drawings. I need samples of work in other media, too. I'll be a senior next year, so that's my last chance to get together the samples I need. And after the turnout for the art fair, I'd say my chances are as slim as ever," he added bitterly.

"I wish we could help," Trixie said in a sympathetic tone.

"Well, thanks," Nick said. "But I don't see how you can. Not unless you know somebody on the school board that you can persuade to give the art department more money. It's a vicious circle. Other departments, like theater and athletics, can raise money by selling tickets to their plays or games. The school board gives them money, knowing they'll earn part of it back. But art just isn't like that. If we'd been able to raise a lot of money here today, there might have been a chance, but—" Nick shrugged.

"If anyone can think of a way to help, it's Trixie,"

Honey assured Nick. "But in the meantime, I can do something, and that's buy the picture of the Manor House. It's perfectly perfect, and it will make the best Mother's Day present I could ever find."

"Oh, woe," Trixie moaned. "Here we go again. I'd already decided that I *have* to have the picture of Crabapple Farm, but giving it away was the furthest thing from my mind. Now that you've said that, I'll feel selfish if I don't give Moms the drawing, but I'll be heartbroken if I have to give it up."

Honey laughed. "Knowing you, Trixie, that drawing will be hanging in the living room of Crabapple Farm before the sun sets on Mother's Day. Anyway, it's not as though you're really giving it up. You'll be able to see it every single day until you move away from home—which won't be for a long time."

"You're right, as usual, Honey," Trixie said, handing Nick her money and taking the drawing. "And besides, if I save all my spare nickels and dimes between now and then, maybe I can offer Nick a commission and ask him to draw another—" Trixie broke off in midsentence as she saw Nick staring over her head toward the entrance to the gym.

Turning around, she saw Ben Riker and three

of his friends. They were swaggering into the gym, and Ben's friends were talking loudly enough for everyone at the art fair to hear.

"Sure would be nice to stop over at Wimpy's for a cola," Mike Larson said.

"Yeah, but our buddy Ben is the only one with a car," Jerry Vanderhoef answered. "And he can't come along because he has to play chauffeur to his cute little cousin and her freckle-faced chum."

Ben looked embarrassed, but he managed to reply in the same sneering tone. "It's just my good deed for the day, pals. I'm much too wonderful a guy to pass up two maidens in distress."

"Oh, yeah?" Mike jeered. He turned to the third boy and pretended to be speaking confidentially as he said loudly, "You know what I think? I think Ben's got a crush on tomboy Trixie."

"Nah," Bill Wright said disdainfully. "I think Ben just likes being a chauffeur. I heard he's going to get himself a little uniform and a cap, just like Tom Delanoy, his uncle's chauffeur, wears."

"Hey, knock it off," Ben said, giving Bill a shove that was meant to look playful but actually had a great deal of force behind it.

"What's the matter, Ben? Does the truth hurt your feelings?" Bill shoved Ben back, knocking him into the table that held the display of pottery that Trixie and Honey had looked at earlier.

29

The girls heard the crash as one of the pieces of pottery shattered on the floor, and they rushed to the table with Nick Roberts right behind them.

At the table, they found Amy staring at her shattered blue vase and trying to hold back her tears.

Honey put her arms around Amy. "Oh, I'm so sorry," she said. "Why, oh, why, did it have to be that vase that broke?"

Amy attempted a wry grin that didn't quite work. "I guess that was a third possibility I hadn't considered," she said. "It looks as though I lost, after all."

After a momentary silence, Ben's friends recovered their mocking attitude.

"Oh, Ben," said Jerry sarcastically, "look what you've done. You're so *destructive!*"

"Clumsy, too," added Bill. "Well, now you can get a broom and a dustpan and do your second good deed for the day—cleaning up this terrible mess! See you around, Ben!" Laughing loudly, the boys left the gym.

Ben, his face flushed, reached into his back pocket and pulled out his wallet. "I guess I broke the stupid thing, so I might as well pay for it. What do I owe you?" he asked Amy.

Nick Roberts stepped between the girl and Ben Riker. "That 'stupid thing,' as you call it, took more time and effort than you've probably ever put into anything. It was a work of art, meant to be looked at and enjoyed, not swept up and thrown into a garbage can in a million pieces. I know your type. You've had everything handed to you on a silver platter, and you think you can bail your way out of anything with money. But this is a loss you can't pay for, any more than you can pay for Amy's hurt feelings."

Amy put her hand on Nick's arm. "He didn't break the vase on purpose, Nick. He was pushed. If he wants to try to make up for it by paying for it, let him. After all, we're here to raise money for the art department. I'd hate to think the vase was a total loss."

Ben Riker took a ten-dollar bill out of his billfold and tossed it onto the table. "You heard her, buddy. Here, you can use this to buy a brand-new lump of clay. Come on, girls. I want to get you two home before you get me into any more trouble." Ben turned on his heel and strode out of the gym. Honey and Trixie, too embarrassed even to look at Nick and Amy, followed him.

The three rode home in strained silence. Ben, still angry at Nick Roberts's tongue-lashing, drove Mr. Wheeler's car fast and recklessly. Trixie, knowing that if she opened her mouth she would say something she'd regret later, gritted her teeth and said nothing. Honey, always trying to soothe hurt feelings, made a few random comments on the weather and schoolwork, but she, too, lapsed into silence when she got no reply.

As they neared the Belden driveway, Honey said, "Ben, why don't you take us both to the Manor House? With Jim, Brian, and Mart all busy, Regan will be happier if Trixie and I exercise at least two of the horses."

Regan was the Wheelers' groom. He was a great friend to the Bob-Whites, but he also had a temper suited to his red hair. The Bob-Whites all tried to do their share of exercising and grooming the horses, to avoid upsetting him. Still, Trixie thought about begging off the ride, afraid that she'd be unable to keep herself from saying something to Honey about Ben's behavior, but she was also afraid of asking Ben to make the extra stop at Crabapple Farm.

The silence between the two girls continued as they went up to Honey's bedroom to change, Trixie into a pair of jeans and a T-shirt borrowed from her friend. They didn't speak during the walk to the stable or while they were saddling Susie and Lady. But the warm spring weather and the first signs of green on the trees of the Wheeler game preserve soon soothed Trixie's temper, and she began to talk about the lack of funds for the art department and what they could do to help.

"I could ask Daddy to make a big donation," Honey suggested. "You know he's always willing to help out in the community. He thinks Sleepyside Junior-Senior High School is a wonderful school because my grades are better here than they ever were before. Although," she said with a sigh, "they still aren't very good."

"I suppose if it comes down to that, you could ask him," Trixie said. "But I'd much rather have the Bob-Whites do something to raise the money. After all, your father isn't a student at Sleepyside, and we are."

Honey giggled at the mental picture of her husky, businesslike father sitting at a school desk, raising his hand to volunteer an answer. "That's true. But what can we Bob-Whites do that we haven't already done? We've had an ice-skating show and an antique show, and we had an auction that wasn't very successful, and—"

"That's it!" Trixie shouted so loudly that Susie, startled, shied, and Trixie had to pause for a moment to calm the horse before she could continue. "That's exactly what we'll do to raise money for the art department: We'll do what we didn't do before!"

Big Plans • 3

HONEY PULLED LADY to a halt and stared at her friend as though she'd just taken leave of her senses. "Why, Trixie Belden," she said, "that's what I just said. Of course we have to do something to raise money for the art department that we haven't done before. That doesn't solve the problem if we don't know what that something is."

"We *do* know what that something is, Honey," Trixie replied. "What I meant was, we'll do what we were *going* to do before but didn't!"

"The walkathon!" Honey exclaimed, finally understanding what Trixie meant. "Oh, what a perfectly perfect idea! We were going to have a walkathon to raise the money to replate Hoppy, but we never did because we donated the reward money we got for finding him—what I mean is, the reward that Sammy almost got, except that he stole Hoppy in the first place and only pretended to find him, so they gave it to us. The money, I mean, and— Why, Trixie Belden, why are you laughing?"

"I'm laughing because your way of explaining things is just as jumbled as mine is," Trixie said between giggles. "It's a good thing we know each other so well, because we'd never be able to understand each other otherwise."

Honey started to giggle, too. "Jim sometimes says, when I've got something hopelessly confused, 'I don't know whether you've been listening to Trixie too long or the other way around, but pretty soon I'm not going to be able to understand either one of you.' Anyway, the important thing is that we're going to raise money for the art department by having a walkathon, right?"

"Wrong," Trixie said. "Not a walkathon. A bike-athon. Right through the game preserve. It's so beautiful right now, with the first leaves on the trees and everything turning bright and green. A lot of the kids at school have asked me what the preserve is like, and I'm sure even more of them have asked you about it, Honey. I'm positive that they'd sign up for the bikeathon just to see it. It has to be a bikeathon because walking on the highway and through the woods is much too dangerous."

"Oh, Trixie, you're wonderful!" Honey exclaimed. "I told Nick Roberts that if anyone could come up with the answer to his problems, it would be you. And I was right! Oh, when do we have it? What do we have to do? What will the route be?"

"Wait a minute!" Trixie said. "I just got the idea. You can't expect me to have all the answers yet. Besides, there's a lot of work involved. We'll need all the Bob-Whites to help. I'll tell Mart and Brian and call Di. You get Jim and Dan." Di and Dan took part in most of the club's activities. Di had grown up in Sleepyside, but she and Trixie hadn't become friends until after Di's father had made a fortune practically overnight and moved his family to a mansion near the Wheelers'. Dan Mangan was Regan's nephew. He'd come to live with Mr. Maypenny, the Wheelers' gamekeeper, after he'd fallen in with a bad crowd in New York City.

"I know Dan and Di will want to help," Honey said, "although they're both busy a lot, with Dan working for Mr. Maypenny and Di baby-sitting for her two sets of twin brothers and sisters. But let's try to meet at the clubhouse after dinner."

"Yipes!" Trixie exclaimed. "Speaking of dinner, I was supposed to help Moms get it ready! Let's get back to the stable and curry the horses and clean the tack so that I can get home before Moms disowns me!"

During dinner, Trixie excitedly explained her plan to her family. They all agreed that it was a good idea to help a very worthy cause.

"I just wish you'd come up with your idea before now, when I'm a senior," Brian said. "Drawing is an excellent way to learn anatomy, which I'll need when I'm studying to become a doctor. But from what I've heard about the art classes at Sleepyside, they just aren't good enough to sacrifice something else I need, like chemistry or math."

Mart Belden helped himself to another portion of mashed potatoes and gravy as he said, "My sagacious elder sibling is never profligate in his predilection for beneficial electives."

Trixie made a face at Mart. "If you mean that Brian doesn't waste his time taking useless classes, you're right. If you followed his example, you'd take three hours a day of spelling so that you could write those big words you love to say."

"You know, Trixie," Mr. Belden said, interrupting his two middle children's verbal spat, "your mother was an art major, and I think she could tell you about the high cost of art supplies."

"Oh, my, yes," Mrs. Belden said. "Even back then, paints and brushes were very expensive. In fact, I practically gave up my artwork when your father and I were first married because we didn't have very much money. And then when you children came along, I got involved with other things, like trying to cook enough food to satisfy five enormous appetites, and I just never got back to painting. I can't begin to imagine how young people afford supplies now, the way prices on everything have increased."

"At least you're not bitter about it, Moms, the way Nick Roberts is." Trixie told her family about the art fair, including both Ben Riker's rude behavior and Nick Roberts's flash of temper.

"I don't know Nick Roberts well enough to tell you why he behaved the way he did," Brian said, "although I have seen him around school. But it sounds to me as though Ben was on the defensive because of the way his so-called friends acted. I don't think Ben is a bad guy. He just needs to do some growing up. Be patient with him, Trix."

"Yeah, Trixie," Bobby, her six-year-old brother, said. "Be nice to Ben. I like Ben. He plays with me an' tells me funny stories, an' one time he even taked me hunting with him and we caught a squirrel that looked like a parrot."

Trixie sighed. "I know, Bobby. Ben has been

nice to you. So I'll try to be nice to Ben. It certainly is hard, though, the way he's been acting lately."

"I heartily concur, my dear Beatrix," Mart said, easing the shock of his agreeing with Trixie by calling her by her hated full name. "Ben Riker's once merely annoying behavior has become downright pernicious. In short, he's really hard to take."

"Well," Trixie said, "I guess we'd better try to take him for a while longer, if only for Honey and Jim's sake. After all, he's Honey's cousin and the Wheelers' guest."

After dinner, the Bob-Whites met at the clubhouse to plan the bikeathon. Trixie and Honey had already filled the others in on the art department's need for money and the general plan, so the seven members began immediately to plan the details.

They quickly decided that the bikeathon should be held as soon as possible, before school let out for the summer and the students were all scattered. The date decided on was two weeks from the following day, a Saturday.

The Bob-Whites also decided that a route covering twenty-five miles would be the right length to ensure that everyone could ride the distance without getting too tired and also be home before dark.

"I know just the route we should take," Dan Mangan said. "Starting at the school, we can go along Old Telegraph Road to the Albany Post Road, then along Glen Road to Lytell's store. Then we can go along the path through the game preserve to Mr. Maypenny's and have a rest stop there. Finally, we'll ride along the other path that goes from Mr. Maypenny's through more of the preserve, between Di's and the Manor House, and back out to Glen Road and into Sleepyside."

"Gleeps, Dan, that's perfect!" Trixie told him. "Maybe we could even have a picnic at Mr. Maypenny's. That would get lots of kids to sign up. We'll need other rest stops, too. I hadn't even thought about those. We could stop at Mrs. Vanderpoel's, I bet. You know how she loves young people. But shouldn't we have another rest stop somewhere along Old Telegraph Road? Does anybody know of a good place?"

The other Bob-Whites shook their heads.

"I'll tell you what," Jim said. "Let's wrap up the other details, then pile into the station wagon and drive along Old Telegraph Road and see if we can find a likely spot."

When the others agreed, Jim took charge to finish the meeting quickly. "Dan, why don't you ask Mr. Maypenny if we can use his clearing for our picnic lunch?" Dan had come to know the Wheelers' game warden quite well, what with living and working with the old man, and he told the other Bob-Whites that he was sure Mr. May-penny would agree.

"Great," Jim said. "Honey, you call Mrs. Van-derpoel and ask her if we can have a rest stop there. Brian, you ask the principal if we can have a sign-up booth after school to get riders. I'll ask Sergeant Molinson for a police escort so that no-body will get hurt by cars on the highways. What's left?"

"Posters!" Trixie exclaimed. "And pledge cards for the riders to give to the people who sponsor them. There should be no problem getting those done. This is for the art department, after all. I'll call Nick Roberts and ask him to help. For once we won't have our usual messy, hard-to-read Bob-White artwork."

"Okay," Jim said. "That's it. All aboard the Bob-White express. Next stop, Old Telegraph Road."

The Bob-Whites climbed into the station wagon that Mr. Wheeler had donated to the club. They drove down Old Telegraph Road, looking for a place that would make a good rest stop. About halfway between Glen Road and Albany Post Road, Di Lynch said, "Look! What's that?"

A gravel drive branched off the road to the north. Tall hedges hid what was along the drive. "We'll pull in and see," Jim said. "If we're lucky, maybe it's the home of one of our classmates whose folks will put up with a whole flock of bike riders for half an hour or so."

Pulling into the driveway, the Bob-Whites saw a large clearing on which stood a deserted-looking frame house and a shed. The windows were covered with sheets of plywood crisscrossed with two-by-fours that were obviously meant to discourage vandals.

"It's perfect!" Trixie said, jumping out of the car. "This clearing is plenty big enough, and it's just the right distance from Sleepyside for the first rest stop. Since nobody lives here, we won't have to worry about disturbing anybody if we use it!"

"Hold on, Trixie," Brian said. "Just because nobody lives here doesn't mean we wouldn't be disturbing anyone. Somebody has to own the place, and we'll have to get permission to use the clearing."

"Brian's right," Jim agreed. "Sergeant Molinson will probably know who the owner is. I'll ask him about it at the same time I ask for a police escort. We can probably persuade the owner to let us use the clearing if we assure him that we'll clean it up after the bikeathon. Now it's getting dark. Let's all go home. Tomorrow's Saturday, so everybody will have time to carry out their assignments. I hereby invite everyone over to the

42

Wheeler boathouse tomorrow evening for a picnic lunch, at which time we will all report our progress."

With shouts of "aye, aye" from Brian and Mart, the Bob-Whites got back into the station wagon for the drive home.

A Ruined Picnic • 4

As soon as Trixie awoke the next morning, she thought about calling Nick Roberts to ask for his help with the artwork for the bikeathon. She raced to the phone, looked up the number, and was about to dial when she realized that it was only eight o'clock. It was too early on a Saturday morning to call someone she hardly knew, she decided. Not everyone had the same busy weekend schedule as the Beldens!

Trixie wrinkled her nose as she put the receiver back in its cradle. *Busy* was hardly the word for it. Mrs. Belden managed to run the bustling household without any outside help. That meant not only feeding and clothing the four children and looking after the mischievous Bobby, but also tending a huge garden in the summer and turning the harvest into canned and frozen fruits and vegetables that the family ate all winter.

Mrs. Belden never complained about the amount of work she had to do, and she was generally understanding when Brian, Mart, and Trixie got involved in projects that made them neglect their chores. After all, she felt, her children were enjoying themselves while helping others; that was hardly something to complain about.

But on Saturdays, Mrs. Belden demanded—and got—the full cooperation of her three oldest children in tackling the major chores that had to be done around the house.

This particular Saturday was busier than most, since the week's fair weather signaled the beginning of spring-cleaning. After breakfast, Brian and Mart went outside to begin cultivating the huge garden behind the house, while Trixie helped her mother clean the inside of the house and tried to keep an eye on her rambunctious younger brother.

"All right, Moms," Trixie said. "The breakfast dishes are done, and the kitchen is spick-and-span. What next?"

"Next," her mother replied, "you should try to call your friend Nick. And after that. . . ." Her mother held out a handful of rags and a bottle of furniture polish.

"I know," Trixie said, "*dust*. But, jeepers, thanks for reminding me to call Nick. It had already slipped through my sievelike mind."

She dialed the number and waited for several rings, but no one answered. "Guess I'll have to try later," she said to herself.

She began polishing the living room furniture, humming to herself as she worked. Trixie always complained about having to do housework, but once she began, she found she didn't mind it. *At least you can see the results of your work right away, getting rid of the dust and seeing the furniture begin to shine,* she thought. *It's not like a math problem, where you struggle to get the answer and then have to wait till class the next day to find out if it's right or wrong.*

Finishing the furniture, Trixie began to dust the frames on the pictures hanging in the living room. She paused in front of a landscape that showed a narrow stream lined with bare-branched willow trees. She'd dusted it every week of her life for years. She'd always noticed the signature, Helen Johnson, which was her mother's maiden name, and the date. But today she found herself really looking at it for the first time.

The sky was cloudy with just a hint of chilly-looking sunlight breaking through, and the water in the stream had the same muted, cloudy look to it. The trees were slender, but their trunks seemed well rounded, sturdy but supple. *It's quite good,* Trixie thought. *Moms must have had a lot of talent as an artist. And then she had to drop it for lack of money. Well, I'm not going to let that happen to Nick Roberts or any of the other gifted kids at Sleepyside. Not if I can help it. Speaking of Nick. . . .*

Trixie tried again to get hold of the young artist, but once again there was no answer.

Even though she interrupted her housework several times to phone, Trixie found that the chores were over and she still hadn't been able to talk to Nick.

"I only hope," Trixie said to her brothers as they walked to the boathouse that afternoon, "that everyone else's missions weren't as impossible as mine."

At the Wheelers', the other Bob-Whites did, indeed, have success to report.

"I called the principal at home," Brian said. "He really likes our idea. He says he knows the art department needs help, but it's a matter of trying to spread too little money over too many activities. This seems like a great solution to him. He says we can have a sign-up booth after school,

47

announcements over the public address system, and whatever else we need."

"Mr. Maypenny's with us, too," Dan reported. "Of course, he had to do some grumbling first, about how easy life is for kids these days, and how if they need money for supplies they should go out and earn it." Dan imitated Mr. Maypenny's scowl as the other Bob-Whites chuckled, recognizing the show of toughness Mr. Maypenny always used to hide his soft heart.

"But finally, after all that grumbling," Dan continued, "he said we could use his clearing, and he asked if he should make up a big batch of his hunter's stew—enough to feed the whole crowd!"

"Yummy-yum!" Di Lynch crowed. "Mr. Maypenny's hunter's stew is simply divine—turnips and parsnips and potatoes and beans and corn—"

"And onions and cabbage and tomatoes, all spiced up with garlic and basil and thyme," Trixie added. "And cooked outdoors. Nobody will drop out of the bikeathon when they know that's the reward!"

"Indeed," Mart said. "But have you pondered the predicament of those unfortunate cyclists who overload their alimentary systems with the succulent comestibles and find themselves unable to persevere in their endeavor?"

"If you mean the riders will eat too much to

ride back to Sleepyside and finish the route, I think you've got it backward," Honey Wheeler told Mart. "After a huge bowl of hunter's stew, you *have* to work it all off! Anyway, now we know that Dan and Brian completed their assignments. I have success to report, too. Mrs. Vanderpoel will be happy to have the bikers stop at her house, and she will also provide refreshments. Nothing so wonderful as hunter's stew, of course—just her own fresh-baked cookies!"

"Gleeps!" Trixie exclaimed. "Mrs. Vanderpoel makes the best cookies in the world! We may have the first bikeathon in history where the bikers will *gain* weight!"

"Ahem." Jim interrupted the Bob-Whites' laughter by clearing his throat importantly. "I have a couple of *minor* triumphs of my own to report, if you don't mind."

The Bob-Whites turned to Jim expectantly, and he continued. "First of all, Sergeant Molinson was helpful, as always, and he has agreed to provide a police escort for the length of the bikeathon route. He also told me who owns the abandoned house on Old Telegraph Road. It's a gentleman by the name of Mr. Matthew Wheeler."

"*Daddy* owns the house?" Honey Wheeler's question rose above her friends' astonished gasps. "But how, Jim? When did he buy it?"

"It seems that the house belonged to a small farm that bordered the game preserve. About a year ago, Dad found out that the owners wanted to retire from the farm and move to town. Of course, he bought the farm immediately, since he'd been wanting to extend his property all the way to the road.

"Needless to say, we have Dad's permission to use the clearing. I asked him about it this afternoon. He doesn't want to open the house, since he's had it boarded up carefully to discourage vandals. But he will supply the refreshments to be served at the first rest stop in the clearing. He's also volunteered to let us have Tom Delanoy's help, and the big car, to pick up any cyclists who get tired or have bike trouble along the route."

"Oh, this whole thing is going to be just perfectly perfect!" Honey said. "Isn't it wonderful how it's all working out?"

"Except that I didn't get hold of Nick," Trixie said gloomily. "Well, I guess I'll just have to try again tomorrow."

"There's still plenty of time, Trix," Jim reassured her. "And speaking of time, I'd say it's time to start our picnic!"

"Second the motion!" exclaimed the always-hungry Mart.

"Wait till you see all the food Miss Trask had

the cook pack for us," Honey said. "I told her anybody would think there were going to be eighty people at this picnic, instead of eight."

"Your math is as bad as ever, Honey," Trixie told her friend. "There are only seven Bob-Whites, remember?"

Honey hesitated a moment before she explained. "I invited Ben to join us, Trix. I told him to come down about half an hour after we did so we'd have time to finish our meeting."

Trixie tried not to let her dislike for Ben Riker show in her face. After all, it was Honey and Jim's picnic.

"The more the merrier, I always say," Brian said cheerfully. "Let's see all that food, Honey."

Trixie was happy to be able to busy herself with unpacking the huge picnic hamper, so that she didn't have to worry about whether Ben Riker would manage to spoil the fun of the picnic.

Miss Trask had in fact provided a huge picnic supper. There was a gallon of freshly squeezed lemonade, a huge bowl of raw vegetables and a carton of dip for munching, two packages of fresh buns, three large hamburger patties ready to be cooked for each of the picnickers, and a chocolate cake for dessert.

While Jim started the fire in the fire bowl that the Bob-Whites had made for their cookouts,

51

Trixie, Honey, and Di set the paper plates and plastic "silverware" out on the table. Then Dan and Mart tended the hamburgers while the others waited, crunching their way through the raw vegetables.

"This raw cauliflower is delicious," Trixie said. "Moms always cooks it with a cheese sauce, and that's good, too, but I've never eaten it this way."

"Isn't it yummy?" Honey picked out a carrot stick and took a bite. "Miss Trask says raw vegetables like these are a much better 'crunchy' food than all those snacks that are fried in oil."

"They don't have as many calories, either," Di Lynch said. Di was the prettiest of the three girls. She had dark, almost blue-black hair that fell to her shoulders and large violet eyes. She was aware of her good looks, and she was far more concerned with watching her figure than Honey and Trixie were with watching theirs.

Dan Mangan deposited a plateful of hamburger patties on the table. "Now that you've saved all those calories on your raw vegetables, you can spend them on these tasty morsels," he said in a teasing way.

Di's talk of low-calorie food was forgotten as she grabbed a hamburger bun, put one of the delicious-looking hamburgers on it, and loaded it down with catsup, mustard, and relish. Trixie,

Honey, and Dan followed suit, and Brian took his turn tending the remaining hamburgers while they finished cooking.

For a few minutes, the only conversation among the young people consisted of mumbled requests for more lemonade or another hamburger and bun.

Just as Brian put the last of the cooked patties on the table and started to construct a hamburger for himself, Ben Riker sauntered up to the table.

"Hi, guys," he drawled. "These eats look good." He helped himself to Brian's hamburger. "Thanks for fixing my burger for me, buddy."

Typical, Trixie thought, *for Ben Riker to show up after all the work is done, when there's nothing left to do except for the easy part—eating.* She looked around at the others in the group. Honey's eyes were lowered to avoid looking at any of her friends. Mart was looking at Ben with thinly concealed outrage. The other Bob-Whites were suddenly concentrating very hard on their food.

Jim broke the silence by telling Ben that the bikeathon looked like a sure thing, thanks to all the cooperation they were getting. Jim said he felt that it was bound to be a big success. "Would you like to ride in the bikeathon, Ben?" he asked.

Ben chewed slowly on a bite of his hamburger for a moment and washed it down with a swallow of lemonade. "I might go along for the ride if it's a nice day. To tell you the truth, though, I'm not very concerned with raising money for your beloved art department. For one thing, I hope to bid good-bye to the sleepy little town of Sleepyside long before school starts next year. And for another thing, I wouldn't knock myself out for any art department. Art students are all just a bunch of dabblers, anyway."

Across the table, Trixie could see her brother Brian giving her a steady, piercing look that meant, "Calm down, Trix, and back off." But it was too late to stop her temper from flaring.

"You can't really believe that, Ben Riker. It's so far from the truth that *nobody* could say something like that and mean it. I think the truth is that you just don't have the talent or the ability to work hard that it takes to be an artist. So you hide behind saying that artists are 'dabblers.'"

Ben Riker looked startled for a moment after Trixie finished her tirade. He opened his mouth as if to answer, then closed it and fixed it in a snide grin. Instead of speaking, he just waved one hand in the same gesture that he would use to brush away a bothersome insect.

Ben's response—or lack of it—made Trixie angrier still, and she probably would have begun another outburst if her brother Brian hadn't interrupted. He yawned broadly and said, "I guess the rest of you didn't spend the whole day in the fresh air plowing up a garden. Mart and I did, and we're tired. I think the Beldens should call it a night."

Mart looked more surprised than tired while Brian was speaking, but then he glanced quickly from Trixie, who looked angry, to Honey and Jim, who looked embarrassed, and realized what his brother was trying to do. He quickly stood up, yawning and stretching, and said, "Indubitably, my dear brother. Your idea is apropos, as always. Coming, Beatrix?"

Trixie rose quickly, muttered a good-night under her breath, and started off toward home.

Her brothers said more lengthy good-bye's and thank-you's, then hurried after her. Brian caught up with Trixie first and threw his arm around her shoulder. "Good old Trixie," he said. "Predictably unpredictable, as usual. When are you going to learn to control your temper?"

"Well, that Ben Riker deserved it!" Trixie said. "He—"

Mart interrupted. "*He* may have deserved it, Trixie. I think he deserves a lot worse than a tongue-lashing. The point is, do Honey and Jim deserve it? Do they deserve to be embarrassed and hurt at their own party? I don't think so. It's not worth trying to get even with Ben Riker if it endangers our friendship with Honey and Jim.

And little outbursts like yours *do* endanger the friendship."

"Oh, Mart, you're right," Trixie moaned. "I couldn't bear it if the Wheelers and the Beldens weren't best friends, especially if I was the cause of it. Nothing Ben Riker could say or do could be worse than losing Jim and Honey. I'll try to remember that. And, Brian, thanks for getting me out of there before I lost my temper some more."

The Beldens walked the rest of the way to their house in silence. Trixie looked at her brothers. *I don't know what they're thinking, but I'm thinking that there's big trouble ahead for the Bob-Whites if Ben Riker stays in Sleepyside.*

Depression • 5

RIGHT AFTER BREAKFAST the next morning, Trixie went to the telephone and dialed Nick Roberts's number. She was thinking, with a chuckle, that she'd already memorized his number without ever actually speaking to him on the telephone, when she heard Nick's voice saying "Hello" on the other end of the line.

"There you are!" Trixie blurted. "I had begun to think that you and your whole family had left town!"

"Who is this?" Nick said. His voice sounded annoyed.

Gleeps! thought Trixie. *There I go again, not*

*using the telephone manners that Moms has tried
so hard to drum into my thick skull. A caller should
always identify himself first thing. Now Nick's
upset, and I can't say that I blame him.*

Aloud Trixie said, "I'm sorry, Nick. This is Trixie
Belden. I met you at the art fair the other day,
remember?"

"Sure. Your friend broke Amy Morrisey's vase,"
Nick said, his voice still chilly.

I can't seem to win, thought Trixie. *The other
Bob-Whites are mad at me because I'm not Ben
Riker's friend. Now Nick is acting angry because
he thinks I am.*

"Well, I didn't call to talk about Ben Riker,"
Trixie told Nick. "I called to tell you that we have
a plan to help the art department raise money.
Would you like to hear about it?"

"Sure," Nick replied. His tone implied that he
doubted whether the plan would be much help.

Trixie drew a deep breath and tried to recall
her earlier enthusiasm. Somehow, Nick's attitude
was causing her to have doubts, too. Nevertheless,
she related the Bob-Whites' plan for the bikeathon
to Nick, telling him about all of the people they'd
already contacted and including the big surprise—
that Mr. Wheeler was the owner of the house
where the Bob-Whites planned to have the first
rest stop. When she finished, she waited breath-

lessly for Nick's response.

There was a long pause before Nick replied. "It sounds as if you have the whole thing worked out," he said finally. "Where do I fit in?"

"We were wondering if you—or someone from the art department—would be willing to make the posters and pledge cards. The posters will be placed around town to get people interested in signing up both as riders and as sponsors. Then, when riders do sign up, they'll be given pledge cards. They'll get different people to sign them, offering to pay so many cents for each mile of the route. After the bikeathon, we contact the people who have signed all the pledge cards, and that's how we collect the money. So you see, the posters and pledge cards are pretty important. Usually we make posters and things ourselves, but in this case, since the money is going to the art department, we felt it was important to have them look sort of—well, artistic—and that's why I'm calling," Trixie finished lamely. She wondered why she felt apologetic about asking Nick to help.

There was another long pause before Nick answered. "I don't have as much spare time on my hands as you and your friends seem to, but if this bikeathon business is supposed to help the art department, I guess I should help out. Talk to me about it in school tomorrow."

"Thanks, Nick. Where should I meet—" Trixie heard a clicking noise and realized that Nick had already hung up. "Well," she muttered, hanging up the phone, "I guess I succeeded in my assignment— *if* I can track Nick down at school tomorrow to talk to him."

Trixie started to walk away from the phone, then snapped her fingers as another thought struck her. She picked up the phone again and dialed Honey's number.

When Honey answered, Trixie told her about Nick's reluctantly agreeing to do the posters and pledge cards, then added, "But guess what we forgot. There are going to be simply loads of kids biking around that route—and we know where it goes, but they don't. We'll have to have arrows up along the roads, pointing the direction. I don't want to ask Nick to do the arrows, too—not after the way he reacted to doing the other stuff. Besides, how artistic does an arrow have to be? I think we should handle those ourselves."

"You're right, Trixie," Honey agreed. "I think we have some poster board and paint down at the clubhouse. I'll be glad to help."

"That's great," Trixie said. "How about meeting me at the clubhouse in an hour?"

"Oh, Trixie, I can't do it today," Honey said apologetically. "My parents are taking Jim, Ben,

and me to a baseball game in the city this afternoon, and then to dinner afterward. I'm sorry."

Trixie once again felt resentment of Ben Riker
welling up inside her. Without stopping to think,
she said sarcastically, "In all the time I've known
you, I didn't realize that you were such a baseball
fan, Honey. At least, I've never known you to let
a baseball game interfere with doing something
worthwhile. I guess I'll just have to take care of
everything alone."

As soon as the words were spoken, Trixie re-
gretted them. For the third time that day, she
found herself waiting uncomfortably for the person on the other end of the telephone to speak.

When Honey did respond, it was in an icy tone
that Trixie had never heard her use before—would
not, in fact, have believed possible from her gentle,
tactful friend.

"Might I point out to you, Trixie Belden, that
all of the other Bob-Whites had their assignments
completed yesterday—before the picnic that you
ruined with your flash of temper. I hardly think
that means you're 'taking care of everything alone.'
Besides, there's an old saying about charity beginning at home that you should pay attention to. You
could devote some time to the worthwhile project
of understanding Ben, instead of plunging into
helping Nick Roberts, whom you hardly know.

"I think you're more worried about getting a lot of attention from organizing the bikeathon than you are about helping anybody. That's what I think." Honey's voice sounded choked as she finished speaking.

For the second time that day, Trixie heard the abrupt clicking sound through the receiver. She blinked back tears as she put the telephone down.

Trixie's hot temper was well-known by all the Bob-Whites. They knew that their friend spoke without thinking—and often without feeling as strongly about things as her words would seem to indicate. For that reason, they tended to respond by teasing Trixie out of her bad mood, rather than taking it seriously. An angry response like Honey's was something that Trixie had rarely had to deal with, and it was all the harder for her to cope with it since it had come from Honey, who seldom became upset with anyone.

Trixie knew that it wouldn't take long for some member of her close-knit family to notice her tearful face and ask her what was wrong. She knew, too, that she didn't want to explain it to her family, especially since her hurt and confusion at Honey's response was mixed with guilt for what she had said.

Trixie swallowed hard and cleared her throat so that her voice would sound relatively steady when she called out, "I'm going to the clubhouse, Moms. I'll be back before dinner." She left the house quickly and started for the clubhouse at a fast trot that made thinking—and crying—impossible to do.

Unexpectedly, the sight of the Bob-Whites' clubhouse made Trixie feel even worse. The tiny building, which had once been the gatehouse of the Wheeler estate, had been donated to the club by Honey's father. Then all of the Bob-Whites had pitched in to turn the run-down building into their "dream house." Jim, Brian, and Mart had put on a new roof and built furniture and shelves to furnish the inside. Honey had sewed the cheerful curtains that framed the windows. All of the Bob-Whites—including Trixie, whose five-dollar-a-week allowance was earned by looking after Bobby and helping her mother with the housework—had worked hard to earn the money for the materials they needed.

The clubhouse served as a meeting hall, storage area, and party room for Trixie and her friends. Trixie associated it with good times and the warm feeling that all of the Bob-Whites had for one another.

I wonder if that's all changed now, Trixie thought, pausing with her hand on the doorknob. *I wonder if Honey will ever speak to me again.*

63

She felt almost like an intruder as she opened the door and walked in. She went to the small storage area that the boys had partitioned off and almost began to cry again when she saw the seven pairs of ice skates jumbled together on a shelf along with the skis, sleds, tents, and other sports equipment that the Bob-Whites shared. *Or used to share,* Trixie thought. She quickly found some poster board, red paint, and a brush and went back to the big table in the middle of the room.

Laying out a piece of poster board and dipping the brush into the paint, Trixie drew the outline of the first arrow. She tried to keep her mind on her work, but as she made the long brush strokes to fill in the arrow, her mind again returned to what Honey had said.

She tried to figure out why Honey had reacted so strongly. Was Honey feeling guilty about neglecting the bikeathon for the baseball game? Was she tired of trying to defend Ben's actions to her friends?

Or maybe, Trixie thought, drawing the outline of another arrow, *she meant exactly what she said. And maybe she's right.* Trixie was the one who always seemed to get the Bob-Whites involved in mysteries and other projects. Was that just coincidence? Or did she get involved because she liked all the attention and the credit for helping people and solving mysteries? She began to wonder about her own motives. *Even a few days ago, at the art fair, when Nick Roberts said I was a celebrity, I felt just as much flattered as embarrassed. . . .*

Trixie's mind kept revolving around the same troubled thoughts as she continued to work, outlining and then filling in red arrows on the poster board.

"Oh, woe," she said finally. "This isn't doing a thing to get my mind off my problems—or to find a solution for them. Indoor work never was my style. I guess I'll go home and get my bike. A little workout will do me good."

As soon as Trixie began pedaling down the Belden driveway, she felt better. The day was one of the best that spring had yet offered. The air was that perfect temperature that felt like no temperature at all, and the hint of breeze was enough to feel good on Trixie's face as she rode, without being hard to pedal against.

Trixie looked at the trees, which had tiny light green leaves beginning to show on the branches.

Spring is finally here, Trixie thought. *Soon it'll be summer, and then we'll—* Trixie's thoughts broke off as she remembered her quarrel with Honey.

What would the summer bring? More adventures, like the ones they'd had sailing off Cobbett's

Island or finding the missing emeralds in Williamsburg? Or were those wonderful summers over for the Bob-Whites?

Feeling the lump begin to rise in her throat once again at the thought of losing Honey's friendship forever, Trixie leaned over the handlebars and began to pedal as fast and as hard as she could.

When she was totally out of breath, she began to coast and raised her head to look around her. To her surprise, she found that she was approaching the deserted house on Old Telegraph Road.

A Piece of Charred Paper • 6

TRIXIE TURNED onto the gravel drive, got off the bike, and pushed the kickstand down with her foot.

For a few moments, she stood still, leaning on the bike seat with one hand while she caught her breath after her wild ride. When she was finally breathing easily again, she began to walk around the clearing.

She paced off the distances and discovered that the clearing was almost one hundred feet wide and fifty feet deep, plenty of room for as many cyclists as would probably be there at one time.

Then Trixie scouted around the clearing, looking at the ground for any pieces of broken glass or rusty nails that could puncture a bike tire—or a bare knee.

There was so little debris on the ground that Trixie decided Mr. Wheeler must have hired someone to come over to the deserted house occasionally and check on it and clean up the grounds.

"There are just too many vandals in the world these days who have nothing better to do than wreck abandoned houses, or at the very least clean out their cars on the front lawns," Trixie muttered.

After Trixie had finished cleaning up the yard and had put what little trash she found in piles to be picked up later, she decided to do a little exploring.

The two-story frame house had once been white, but most of the paint had peeled away years before, leaving the boards underneath to weather. There was a small brick stoop on the front of the house, and on the stoop sat an old concrete urn that was filled with caked and lumpy dirt and a few dried stems of long-dead plants.

As Trixie walked around to the back of the house, she saw that all of these windows had been covered with sheets of plywood and crisscrossed with two-by-fours, like those in the front.

"When Mr. Wheeler wants to protect an abandoned house, he goes all the way," Trixie said aloud. "It'd take more than a casual vandal to break into this place. A person would have to have a lot of determination even to try."

In the back, Trixie discovered that the house had an old-fashioned cellar, with the heavy wood doors to the outside built parallel to the ground. The wood was weathered and splintered from being covered with snow and rain, but the sturdy brass hinges still looked shiny. "I bet they'd turn without so much as a squeak if someone pulled open that door," Trixie said to herself. "It's too bad there's no way to find out." The doors were locked with a massive padlock.

When she'd seen what little there was to see around the house, Trixie turned her attention to the backyard. The outlines of the dilapidated picket fence indicated that it had been a huge yard —although now it was difficult to distinguish the yard from the game preserve beyond it, since both were covered with rough grass and weeds.

In one corner of the yard, an area surrounded by wire fence indicated what had once been the garden. Trixie wandered over to it to see if anything had come up "volunteer" this spring, but so far only a few small weeds and the first sprigs of spreading grass had invaded the garden.

As Trixie turned to walk back to her bike, she was forced to admit that this was the most unmysterious abandoned house she'd ever seen. Even if she hadn't known the background, about the former owners' moving to town and Mr. Wheeler's buying it from them, she didn't think she would have found a single thing to make her suspect a mystery.

That's just as well, Trixie thought as she pedaled back down the drive. *My mysteries have gotten me into enough trouble lately. I almost wish I'd never dig up another one, in fact.*

Trixie had ridden only about a quarter of a mile when she saw a piece of paper that had been blown against a hedge along the road.

There's the kind of litter I was looking for, she thought. She stopped her bike and walked down the shallow ditch to the hedge. Picking up the piece of paper, she noticed that it was charred around the edges. Exposure to rain and sun had aged it, too, so that it was difficult to read.

The piece of paper was about the size of one of the coupons that Trixie sometimes clipped from magazines for her mother, the kind that offered five or ten cents off the price of a brand of food or a household cleaner.

"It's a lot prettier than a coupon, though," Trixie muttered, holding the piece of paper close to her face to inspect it. On one side, the paper showed a picture of a quaint-looking man wearing a furry hat, with a furry collar pulled up close around his face. On the other side was a huge castle that looked like something out of a fairy tale.

"It looks like a picture out of a book, except for those red numerals running across the bottom and the numeral *fifty* printed in the corners. I wonder what it is and how it got out here in the middle of nowhere." After staring at the piece of paper for a few more moments, Trixie sighed and put it in her pocket. "I'm not going to be able to figure it out just by thinking about it," she decided. "I'll take it home and see if Mart or Brian knows what it is. If not, it'll make a good addition to Bobby's 'collection.'"

Trixie smiled as she walked back to her bike, thinking about her younger brother's "collection," which was actually a random assortment of anything the six-year-old happened to find interesting, including buttons, marbles, bubble gum cards, and any number of other oddities.

When Trixie returned to Crabapple Farm, she discovered that her bike ride had taken longer than she thought. The aroma of Mrs. Belden's New England boiled dinner, with cabbage and onions dominating the corned beef, carrots, and celery, filled the air.

"Yipes, Moms, I'm sorry!" Trixie apologized. "I was supposed to help with dinner tonight, and you've had to do it all yourself."

"I've just done the easy part, Trixie," Mrs. Belden replied. "I chopped up some vegetables and put them in the pot to simmer with the meat and took some rolls out of the freezer and put them in the oven to warm up. I managed to save the hard part for you—getting your younger brother cleaned up and ready for the table."

Trixie giggled. " 'Hard part' is right," she said. "It would be easier to put together a gourmet feast than it is to hold Bobby still long enough to get a whole day's worth of grime off his hands and face."

Sure enough, Bobby started to protest with the first swipe of the washcloth. "Ouch, Trixie!" he hollered. "That hurted me! You only have to take the dirt off—not my skin!"

Trixie sighed. "Bobby, the problem is that you get the dirt so ground in that it's hard to tell which is dirt and which is skin." Remembering the piece of paper in her pocket, Trixie said, "I'll tell you what, Bobby. If you let me finish cleaning you up without saying one more word, and if you eat one whole cooked carrot at dinner tonight, I'll give you a surprise."

"Oh, boy!" Bobby exclaimed. "A s'prise! What is it, Trixie?" In his excitement, Bobby had become wigglier than ever.

"If I tell you, I'll spoil the surprise. Is it a deal?" she asked, doing her best to sound businesslike, although her little brother's wide-eyed excitement made her want to giggle, instead.

"One whole cooked carrot is a lot, Trixie," Bobby said seriously. "I don't like to eat even one bite of cooked carrot." He considered the bargain for a moment. Finally he said, "Okay, Trixie, it's a deal." He took a deep breath and shut his eyes so tightly that his button nose wrinkled.

It took Trixie a second to figure out the reason for the terrible face Bobby was making. She suppressed another giggle as she realized that he was preparing to carry out the first part of his bargain, to let Trixie finish washing his face without any more protests.

Trixie was able to finish the clean-up operation quickly once Bobby's cooperation was insured. "There you go, sport," she said. "All finished."

Bobby let out his breath, opened his eyes, and blurted, "One *small* cooked carrot. Okay, Trixie?"

Laughing, Trixie gave her brother a hug and hurried him downstairs.

Bobby and Trixie got to the dining room to see Mart coming in from the kitchen with the huge platter of cooked vegetables and meat. Brian was right behind him with a basket of rolls.

"Moms told us we could eat as soon as you

helped her put the food on the table," Brian said, his eyes twinkling. "Somehow, the idea of having to wait for dinner until you finished scrubbing the backyard from our youngest sibling's face made Mart forget that carrying food is 'woman's work.'"

"I did not forget," Mart said haughtily as he set down the platter of vegetables and took his place at the table. "I simply allowed the lure of the repast to overcome my abhorrence for menial tasks."

"Serving food is not a menial task," Trixie said as she sat down. "As a matter of fact, it isn't even necessarily women's work. Honey says—" Trixie felt a pang as she remembered her fight with Honey, about which her family knew nothing. She felt herself redden as she continued. "Honey says that when she and Jim and their parents go to the fancy restaurants in New York, the food is almost always served by waiters. So there, Mart Belden."

Mrs. Belden chuckled. "I would suggest that we all serve ourselves, now that the food is on the table, before it gets cold. But first, Brian, since your father is out of town for a couple of days, why don't you ask the blessing?"

The Beldens all bowed their heads while Brian said a short prayer of thanks. Trixie listened with her head lowered, thinking how mature her oldest brother's voice was beginning to sound. It was easy to imagine him as a doctor, giving people all sorts of sound medical advice in that quiet, confident voice, she thought.

As soon as the family said "amen," a distinctly immature voice was heard. "Pass me the vegetables first, please," Bobby piped.

Bobby's mother and his brothers looked at him in astonishment as Trixie, straight-faced, handed him the vegetables.

"To what may we attribute young Robert Belden's sudden conversion to vegetarianism?" Mart asked, looking at Trixie suspiciously.

"I just explained how healthful and nutritious they are, Mart," Trixie said teasingly.

"Huh-uh, Trixie," Bobby said helpfully. "That's not what you 'splained. You 'splained that if I would eat a whole cooked carrot, you would give me a s'prise after dinner. And I asked for the vegetables first 'cause I want the very smallest carrot."

Brian, Mart, and Mrs. Belden burst into laughter, and Trixie joined in, while Bobby looked from one to the other, trying to understand what was so funny.

After dinner, Trixie kept her promise and gave the piece of paper to Bobby.

"What is it, Trixie?" he asked.

"I don't know, Bobby," she said. "It's just a funny-looking piece of paper."

75

"May I see it, Bobby?" Brian asked. "I'll give it right back." He took the piece of paper and looked at it.

Mart looked at the paper over Brian's shoulder and said immediately, "That funny-looking piece of paper is in fact a fifty-deutsche-mark note."

"D-Doich what?" Trixie asked.

"Deutsche mark, Trixie," Brian said. "That's the basic unit of German currency. It's sort of like our dollar. One deutsche mark is worth about fifty cents in United States' money.

"That piece of paper is therefore worth approximately twenty-five dollars, although I doubt whether you could find anyone who would redeem such a damaged specimen."

"It isn't a specimen," Bobby protested. "It's a s'prise, and it's mine. Trixie gave it to me. May I be 'scused so I can go put my s'prise in with my collection, Moms?"

Mrs. Belden turned to Trixie, who looked stunned by the news that her funny-looking piece of paper was worth twenty-five dollars.

Trixie looked at her mother, smiled, and shrugged.

"You may be excused, Bobby," Mrs. Belden said. When he had left the room, she told Trixie, "I'm sure that once the 's'prise' wears off, Bobby will be willing to try to redeem the money and give you half of it as a finder's fee."

"Maybe," Trixie said ruefully. "But even if he doesn't, I haven't really lost anything, since I probably would have just thrown it away." She turned to her older brothers. "How did both of you happen to know what it was?"

"Elementary, my dear Trixie," Mart said smugly.

"Actually, Trixie, I saw a picture of a fifty-deutsche-mark note just recently," Brian said. "It was in one of Dad's banking magazines. Unfortunately, I didn't read the article that went with the picture, and I couldn't begin to tell you which magazine it was."

"Perhaps your father will remember when he gets home on Wednesday," Mrs. Belden said. "Meanwhile, there are dishes to be done. Trixie—"

"I know," Trixie said. "It's Mart's turn to help, but he helped set the table, so I—"

"Should kindly volunteer to take my turn with dishes," Mart concluded, getting up from the table. "Thanks, Sis."

While she was drying the dishes, Trixie thought about the bank note, wondering how a piece of German money had wound up blown against a hedge on Old Telegraph Road. The *Sleepyside Sun,* like most small-town newspapers, kept careful track of local comings and goings, and if someone in the area had taken a tour of Germany, the paper would certainly have reported it. Trixie couldn't remember any mention of such a trip.

Of course, I might not have paid any attention to the article at the time, Trixie thought as she folded her dish towel. *Maybe Honey would know.*

Trixie walked to the phone and picked up the receiver before she remembered the bad feeling that had surfaced between her and her best friend.

Gleeps, she thought. *I'm so used to confiding everything in Honey that it's impossible to remember that—* She felt a sinking feeling in her stomach as she realized what she'd been thinking—that she and Honey might, in fact, not be best friends anymore.

She stared at the dial for a few seconds, wondering if she should try to call Honey anyway. Hanging up the telephone, she thought, *I can't do it—not tonight. I guess I'm just a coward after all. I can't stand the idea of calling and having Honey refuse to speak to me—or still be as angry as she was this morning.*

Trixie hung up the phone and wandered upstairs to her room. Trying to find something to occupy her restless mind, she leafed through some magazines, tried to get interested in a book, and finally went to her dresser and began cleaning out the drawers.

A few moments later, Mart wandered by and saw Trixie neatly refolding sweaters and arranging them in the top drawer. He knocked on the already-open door and came into the room.

"I deduce," he said, "that my younger sister is in the throes of a peculiar psychological condition, which seems to manifest itself in trying to achieve order in the chaos that is her room. To what, might I ask, may we attribute this odd—albeit welcome—situation?"

"Oh, Mart," Trixie moaned, "what am I going to do?" She told Mart all about her fight that morning with Honey, including Honey's charge that Trixie was more interested in getting attention for herself than in helping others.

To Trixie's surprise, her usually quarrelsome brother listened patiently and, when she had finished, responded soberly.

"I'm really sorry, Trix," he said. "It seems to me that everything has gone topsy-turvy since that Ben Riker came to Sleepyside. I know this sounds cruel, but I wish he'd either straighten up or do something really bad, so that he'd be sent away."

Mart scowled, and Trixie found the corners of her mouth turning up in a smile as she realized that his face was probably the image of the way her own had looked all evening. Mart and Trixie looked enough alike to be taken for twins.

"Anyway," Mart continued, "as for what Honey said about you— Well, Trixie, it's true, at least in part. Everybody wants praise and encouragement from others. That's just human nature. It explains why Ben and his crowd make trouble: They get encouragement and praise from each other for it. The difference is that your acts are intended to help others, and that, my dear sister, is nothing to be ashamed of."

Trixie looked at the floor as tears welled up in her eyes at Mart's gentle words.

Mart stood up and walked toward the door. "Don't worry about your spat with Honey," he said. "I have a feeling it won't last. You two girls are too close for that. 'Night."

"Good night, Mart," Trixie said. "And thanks."

Mart is wonderful, Trixie thought. *For all his teasing, he's not afraid to show he cares about me when I need to know it. And he's right. The fight between Honey and me won't last, because I won't let it. Tomorrow morning on the bus I'll walk right up to her and apologize.*

Posters and Apologies • 7

THE NEXT MORNING, Trixie was waiting eagerly at the bus stop at the foot of the driveway when the school bus arrived. She felt a sinking feeling of disappointment when the bus passed the stop at Manor House and neither Honey nor Jim got on. She slumped down into her seat, wondering if the Wheelers had not taken the bus because they were deliberately avoiding her. *Don't be silly,* she told herself. *There are lots of times when we don't take the bus for one reason or another.* Still, she felt uneasy and nervous, and she looked enviously at Mart and Brian, who were kidding with a group of classmates at the front of the bus.

On her way to her first class, Trixie saw Nick Roberts coming down the hall. He seemed to be looking right at her, but he turned suddenly and started to walk down another corridor before she could speak. *I guess he didn't see me after all*, she thought, hurrying to catch up with him.

"Nick," she called out as she ran up alongside him. The young artist took a couple more steps, then stopped, but he still didn't turn to face her.

"I'm sorry if I distracted you from what you were thinking about," Trixie said apologetically. "I was just wondering when you can work on the posters. I want to arrange for a sign-up booth after school, and I—"

"Forget it," Nick said.

Trixie thought at first that he meant she should forget about apologizing, but as Nick continued to stare at the floor, she wasn't so sure. "Forget what?" she asked.

"Forget the whole thing—the whole stupid bike-athon idea," Nick said angrily. "I don't have time to waste doing a bunch of stupid posters and pledge cards for a bunch of do-gooders. It's a dumb idea, anyway. You probably won't raise any money, and if you do, the school board will just use that as an excuse to cut the art department's budget back even more. We'll be right back where we started."

"Oh, Nick, I don't think so—" Trixie began to reassure him.

"Well, I do," Nick retorted. "And I'm the one who's in the art department, so I ought to know. Just forget the whole thing, would you?" With that, Nick pushed his way past Trixie and walked quickly off down the hallway.

Trixie looked at his retreating figure, too stunned to move. Nick hadn't been exactly enthusiastic about the bikeathon when she'd described her plans the day before, but there certainly had been nothing in his manner to indicate that he was going to decide against the entire project.

Trixie felt a strong temptation to take Nick's advice and abandon the whole idea of helping the art department. So far, she had to admit, it had caused her nothing but trouble and hurt feelings. But, remembering the disappointed looks on the faces of the other young students at the art fair, Trixie felt her resolve returning.

The principal offered us his full cooperation, Trixie thought. *That means it can't be such a bad idea. As long as we've gone this far, we might as well continue. I'll go talk to the art teacher during my study hall.*

To Trixie's relief, the young art teacher, whose name was Mr. Crider, was very friendly and welcomed Trixie's offer to help. He listened closely as

Trixie explained the arrangements that the Bob-Whites had made so far and nodded agreeably when Trixie explained the need for posters and pledge cards.

"I have two classes of first-year art students," Mr. Crider said. "I can give them the posters and pledge cards to do as an assignment. Actually, it will be very good experience for them to do something like this. It will teach them how to take a basic piece of communication and turn it into something attractive. If any of them decide to go into commercial art, that will be a valuable thing for them to know."

"Thanks, Mr. Crider," Trixie said. "If you'll just let me know when they're ready, I'll come back to pick them up." She started toward the door.

"Hold on a minute," Mr. Crider said, chuckling. "My students can't communicate your message very effectively if they don't know what it is. I need to know the date, the time, the place, and what you think is most important to say—what will grab people's attention."

"Of course," Trixie said. "I'm sorry. I have a bad habit of assuming that other people know all the details of things I'm involved in, just because I spend all my time thinking about them."

"That's a fairly common habit with us human beings, Trixie," Mr. Crider assured her. He handed her a piece of paper and a pencil. "That's why someone invented the writer's rough."

Mr. Crider explained that Trixie should make a rough sketch of what she thought the posters and pledge cards should look like, printing out the information and indicating where any special artwork should go.

"Let's see. . . ." Trixie thought for a moment, then wrote a headline, "Come Along for the Ride," and filled in the information about the time and starting point for the bikeathon, as well as the fact that the money raised would be used to help buy supplies and equipment for the art department. "I think we should have a map, too," Trixie said, "so that people who look at the poster will see right away that the route goes through the Wheelers' game preserve. Lots of kids will sign up just to get a chance to tour the preserve." She sketched the map on the paper, then added, "Oh, yes! There's an important line I left out." On the paper, she lettered, FREE REFRESHMENTS WILL BE SERVED.

Trixie then did another writer's rough for the pledge cards and handed the two pieces of paper to Mr. Crider.

The art teacher looked them over and said, "These look fine, Trixie. I'll give them to the first-year students this afternoon, and you should be able to pick up the posters and pledge cards about this time on Wednesday morning."

Trixie thanked him and started to leave, then hesitated. "Mr. Crider, I'm not trying to pry, but I was wondering about Nick Roberts. I don't know him well. Actually, I don't think I know him at all. I was just wondering why he always seems so— well, so troubled. He has so much talent that I'm sure he'll be very successful someday, and he's very attractive, but he always seems so *gloomy*."

Mr. Crider sighed. "I don't know Nick well either, Trixie, despite the fact that he spends all of his free time in this department. I do know that he's had some unfortunate experiences. Nick and his family moved to Sleepyside just last year from New York City. His mother's health isn't very good, and her doctor suggested it might improve if she were away from the pollution of the city.

"Nick's father is a master engraver, and he was in demand in the city, but there isn't much call for his talents in a small town like Sleepyside. He has a little shop downtown, where he sells engraved trophies and plaques and such, but there isn't much money in it. And, although Mrs. Roberts's health has improved since they moved here, the medical bills that they ran up have put them pretty deeply in debt.

"Nick tries to help out by working evenings and weekends as a sign painter, and he does make enough money to pay for his expenses and help out a little with the bills at home. Still, he resents having to take so much time away from his serious work, and, understandably, he's a little bit bitter. I've tried to draw him out since he's been in my classes, but it doesn't seem to work. He's a very unhappy young man, and that's too bad, since, as you said, he does have a lot going for him and will probably succeed eventually—if the chip on his shoulder doesn't stand between him and success."

Trixie nodded soberly. "I understand him a lot better now, Mr. Crider. I'm glad you told me about Nick's background. He must feel as though he's carrying the weight of the whole world around on his shoulders. Still, that's when a person needs friends most."

"I couldn't agree with you more, Trixie," Mr. Crider said. "I hope you'll keep trying to be friends with Nick. Just don't take it too personally if he's not always very open with you."

Trixie thanked Mr. Crider again for his help, and, promising to come back on Wednesday to pick up the posters and pledge cards, she returned to her study hall. On the way, she thought about what the art teacher had said about Nick Roberts.

She realized that Nick had his own artwork to do, and sign painting besides, so it was probably true that he didn't have time to help with the bikeathon. But she couldn't see why he hadn't just explained that to her, instead of getting so angry.

It occurred to her that Nick might have been worrying about something else when she called out to him, and he might have taken out his worry by speaking angrily to her. Or, she guessed, he might have felt guilty because he knew he'd get what he needed out of the bikeathon, but he didn't have time to help.

One thing I know for sure, Trixie concluded. *It's easier to find missing necklaces and lost trailers than it is to figure out why people act the way they do sometimes.*

When Trixie boarded the school bus that afternoon, she saw Honey sitting alone in one of the double seats at the back of the bus. Taking a deep breath to calm her nerves, Trixie quickly walked the length of the bus and sat down in the vacant seat next to Honey.

"Hi," Trixie said. "I got Mr. Crider, the art teacher, to help out with the artwork we need. He says we can pick up the posters and pledge cards Wednesday, so we might as well ask the principal if we can have our sign-up booth right after school Wednesday." Trixie faltered when she saw that Honey's face was set in an unfriendly expression. "I—I guess I should ask if you're still interested in helping with the bikeathon."

"I certainly *am* interested in the bikeathon," Honey replied icily. "*Someone* has to make sure that nothing *else* goes wrong."

"Has something gone wrong, Honey?" Trixie asked. "Did your father withdraw his permission to use the clearing, or—"

"You know perfectly well what I'm talking about, Trixie Belden," Honey interrupted. "I went over to the clubhouse last night after we got home from the city. I wanted to see how far you'd gotten on the direction arrows.

"What I *found* was that you'd left the brush unwashed and the window open, and the jar of red paint had tipped over and spilled all over the table and the top poster. It took me half an hour to clean up the mess, and there's still a red stain on the table."

Trixie stared at Honey open-mouthed. She tried to remember her actions of the day before. Trixie didn't think she'd left the supplies sitting out, but she couldn't remember putting them away, either. She didn't even remember opening the window in the clubhouse, let alone closing it. She finally had to admit to herself that she must have left everything sitting out when she decided to go for the bike ride.

"I'm sorry, Honey," she said in a low voice, not daring to look her friend in the eye. "I must have left the mess that you had to clean up. I didn't do it on purpose. It's just that I was so upset about our fight. That's all I thought about yesterday, all day long. I kept wondering whether we'd ever be friends again, and about what I'd do if we weren't. I guess that's why I forgot to put things away." Trixie felt tears welling in her eyes, and her voice choked as she said, "I'm sorry you had to clean up the mess, and I'm sorry I said such awful things to you yesterday, Honey."

"Oh, Trixie," Honey wailed, "I'm sorry, too! I said perfectly horrid things to you. And I was just as upset yesterday as you were. I should have realized that that's why you left the supplies sitting out. Why, do you know what I did yesterday?"

"What?" Trixie asked, still feeling tearful.

"I was trying to pretend to watch the baseball game so that my family wouldn't know about our fight. But really I wasn't paying any attention at all. I was just staring at the baseball field, not really seeing it, when suddenly everyone started to cheer. I saw a runner crossing home plate, and I jumped up and yelled, 'Touchdown!'"

Trixie's tears turned to giggles. "Oh, Honey," she gasped, "you didn't!"

Honey nodded solemnly, then she began to giggle, too. "And that's not all, Trixie. When I jumped up, I forgot that I had a glass of pop in my hand, and I emptied the whole glassful of cold, sticky pop on Ben's head! You should have seen the look on his face."

In her mind's eye, Trixie *could* see the look on Ben's face: full of anger he couldn't vent because Honey's parents were there, and also full of confusion and bewilderment at seeing his normally poised and tactful cousin acting so foolish.

"Oh, Honey," Trixie said between her giggles, "we don't *dare* fight anymore. It's too dangerous!"

"I agree with you, Trixie," Honey said more seriously. "Fighting with you makes me feel too horrible. Let's never fight again."

"I was all set to apologize this morning," Trixie told Honey. "Then, when you weren't on the bus—"

"Oh, Trixie, I know," Honey said. "Jim has decided we should start riding with Ben. He thinks it might keep him out of trouble. I had to go along with it this morning because I didn't want Jim to know we'd had a fight. Jim's riding home with Ben, too, but I just refused. I *had* to talk to you and try to straighten things out."

"Well, everything's straightened out now," Trixie said emphatically. "Let's not do anything to *un*-straighten it, ever again."

"It's a deal," Honey said. "I'll finish doing the direction arrows, since you started them. Then both of us can work at the sign-up booth Wednesday while the boys take the posters out and put them up. I'll call Di—she wasn't in school today—to find out if she can help.

"Then we can—oops! Here's my stop, Trixie. I'll call you after supper!" Honey gathered up her books and dashed for the door of the bus.

As the bus pulled away, Honey stood in her driveway and waved good-bye to Trixie.

I feel as wonderful this afternoon as I felt awful this morning, Trixie thought as she got off the bus at Crabapple Farm. *Honey and I are friends again.*

"Yippee!" she shouted, running up the driveway to the house.

The Sign-Up • 8

On Wednesday, during her study hall, Trixie went back to the art department to pick up the posters and pledge cards from Mr. Crider.

Trixie was delighted with the work. "How did you do them?" she asked. "They're all so uniform. They look more like something that came off a printing press."

"They *were* done with a printing technique, Trixie," Mr. Crider told her, "although they weren't put on a press. The technique is called *serigraphy,* or silk screening. Would you like to see how it's done?"

When Trixie nodded eagerly, Mr. Crider led

her to a small room in the back of the art department. "Here's where we work," Mr. Crider said. "The process is called silk screening because, as you can see, we use a piece of silk cloth that's been stretched tight on a wooden frame.

"We make a stencil of the artwork, cutting out any places where we want ink to show through on the finished piece. Laying the stencil down on the piece of silk, we paint over the openings with a black, waxy substance." Mr. Crider showed Trixie the stencil that had been used for her posters, putting it down on the silk screen to demonstrate.

"After it dries for half an hour or so, we prepare a mixture of glue and cold water—about a fifty-fifty ratio. We spread the glue mixture over the screen with a squeegee, which is a flat rubber blade like the ones a gas station attendant uses to wash car windows.

"We let the first coat of glue dry, then we apply a second coat and let that dry.

"Finally, we use kerosene and a stiff scrub brush to wash the waxy substance off the areas of the screen where we want the ink to go through, and the screen is ready to use," Mr. Crider concluded.

"Whew!" Trixie exclaimed. "That really sounds complicated!"

"The preparation of the screen is fairly demanding," Mr. Crider admitted, "but once it's ready, the silk-screening process itself is quite simple. All we have to do is pour a generous quantity of paint on one end of the stencil and work it across to the other with the squeegee. As long as the screen and the surface we're printing on are held steady, there's not too much that can go wrong."

"That's a lot better than our system of doing each poster by hand," Trixie admitted. "Sometimes if two or three of us each do a poster, it's hard to tell that they're all supposed to be the *same* poster."

Mr. Crider chuckled. "Next time you have a project like that to do, I'd suggest that you go to the library and take out a book on silk screening. There are several books that show beginners how to get started. You don't really need all of this complicated equipment, either. Some of the easier methods use plain brown wrapping paper instead of wax and glue. If your design is simple enough, you can just put the wrapping paper over your screen. The first coat of paint acts as a kind of glue to keep the paper on the screen where you want it."

"I think we could manage that," Trixie said. "I can think of a lot of ways we could use silk screening. We could even make our own Christmas cards."

"You could indeed," Mr. Crider said. "Silk screening is a very adaptable technique. It came

95

from China, as you might expect, because it uses silk. The Chinese and Japanese used it for making pieces of fine art. Since it came to this country, though, it's found a lot of uses in industry.

"One of its big advantages is that the surface that's being printed on doesn't have to bear much weight—unlike surfaces that have to be put through a printing press. That means that breakable items, like glassware, can be silk screened.

"Well, this is my free period, and I really shouldn't be using it to give a lecture on art," Mr. Crider concluded. "Here are your posters, and I hope you find ways of using silk screening for future projects. Don't hesitate to call me if you need help."

"Thanks, Mr. Crider," Trixie said. "I'll remember your offer!"

After school, the seven Bob-Whites met in front of the principal's office, where the school custodian had already set up a table and chairs for the sign-up.

Jim, Brian, Dan, and Mart divided up the posters and quickly decided which territory each should cover. Brian had driven his jalopy to school that morning, and Jim had the Bob-White station wagon, so they were to cover the shops and businesses farthest from the school. Dan Mangan would take places closest to the school, while Mart put posters up in the hallways of the school itself.

By the time the boys left on their rounds, a number of students had already begun to gather around the sign-up table, thanks to an announcement that had been made over the PA system that afternoon.

Time and again for the next hour, Honey, Trixie, and Di explained to eager students how the bikeathon would work:

"Just take one of these cards and fill in your own name and address. Then take the card to all your neighbors, friends, and relatives, and ask them if they'd be willing to pledge a certain amount of money for each mile you ride—say, five or ten cents. Have them fill in their name and address where it says 'sponsor,' along with the amount they want to pledge per mile.

"We'll have a table set up right here again next Wednesday so that we can collect your cards and hand out more. After the bikeathon, we'll call all the people who signed your cards, telling them how many miles you rode and how much they owe. Then they'll send the money to the school, in care of the art department. That's all there is to it!"

Trixie was in the middle of explaining the bikeathon for the umpteenth time when she spotted Ben Riker and his friends walking up to the table.

Oh, woe, Trixie thought. *I hope they don't make any trouble.*

The boys paused a short distance from the table and watched silently for a moment. Although they said nothing, the smirks on their faces made it clear that they were not about to sign up for the ride or pledge any money for any of the riders.

"You know, guys," Jerry Vanderhoef said finally, "that isn't such a bad idea." His friends looked surprised, but he continued. "I could use some extra spending money, couldn't you? Maybe we should have a bikeathon, too. We could ask for contributions to our favorite charity."

"Yeah—us!" Mike Larson agreed.

"That's right," Bill Wright added. "We could call ourselves 'The Society for the Preservation of Wimpy's Hamburgers.' How's that?"

"There's just one problem with that idea, chums," Ben Riker said. "*This* bikeathon is being run by one of Sleepyside's most illustrious detectives, Supersleuth Trixie Belden. If she got word that you guys were planning to raise money for a cause that wasn't worthwhile, she'd track you down and have you thrown in the slammer. And I *don't* think that dear Miss Trixie would consider raising money for your after-school hamburgers very worthwhile."

Trixie felt her face burning with embarrassment

as the boys kept up their banter. She wanted desperately to say something to the boys, to make them go away, but she remembered how much more miserable she'd been during her brief fight with Honey and resolved to hold her tongue.

Trixie sneaked a look at her friend to see how Honey was reacting to the taunts of Ben and his friends. Honey was explaining the sign-up process to a couple of students. She was trying to look as though she didn't hear what Ben was saying, but she wasn't succeeding. She, too, was flushed with embarrassment, and her usually tranquil-looking face was drawn and pinched.

She's really suffering, Trixie thought. For the first time, Trixie fully realized how hard the situation was for Honey to cope with. Honey felt sympathy for Ben because she knew all too well how lonely his life was. At the same time, she knew that he was choosing the most destructive way possible of dealing with his loneliness.

She doesn't know how she should feel about Ben, Trixie thought. *She just knows that she can't ignore him, because he is her cousin. She's probably waiting, just as Mart is, for Ben to do something so awful that the Wheelers will have to admit defeat and send Ben away for good. If that happens, Honey will always feel guilty because she wasn't able to give him the help he needed.*

With the full realization of Honey's discomfort came full understanding of how much worse Trixie's own behavior had made Honey feel. Trixie had been forcing Honey to choose between her best friend and her conscience. *If she cut Ben off now in order to please me, and then Ben went off the deep end, she'd hate herself, and, what's more, she'd hate me, too.*

Trixie knew that it would be easier for her to tolerate Ben Riker from now on.

Ben and his friends finally tired of their taunts and moved on, and shortly afterward the last of the students interested in the bikeathon left the table, pledge cards in hand.

Fortunately, Ben's rude behavior hadn't dampened the enthusiasm of the students at the booth, nor had it given them cause to doubt the good intentions behind the bikeathon. Mart had taped one of the posters on the wall next to the table, and the map of the bikeathon route had been a strong selling point, as Trixie had known it would be. She'd heard many of the students talking among themselves about how interesting it would be to see the Wheeler game preserve firsthand. Trixie smiled to herself as she remembered the second most common remark she'd overheard: "Look! There are going to be free refreshments, too!" She knew that most of them would be expecting the usual unimaginative hot dogs and hamburgers.

"Won't they be surprised," she said aloud to Honey and Di, "when they show up at Mr. Maypenny's and discover that huge kettle of hunter's stew?"

"We really should tell them about it in advance," Di said. "Otherwise, they'll eat so many of Mrs. Vanderpoel's delicious cookies that they'll have to go around the bike route all over again to work up an appetite!"

"How many people signed up?" Trixie asked.

Honey finished counting the lists of names and looked up with a wide smile. "There are already fifty riders, Trixie, with more to come!"

Trixie did some fast calculating. "Let's see. If we have fifty riders, and they each get a dollar a mile in pledges. . . . Gleeps! That will be over a thousand dollars for the art department!"

"Oh, Trixie, that's wonderful!" Honey exclaimed. "Are you sure?"

Di Lynch had been figuring with paper and pencil. "That's right, Honey. See?" She showed the figures to Honey and Trixie. "Trixie only has trouble with math problems in class. When it comes to one of her pet projects, she has no trouble at all."

"That's what I've been trying to tell everybody, especially when I bring home my report card.

There's nothing wrong with my answers in math class. It's the problems that are wrong!"

Still laughing at Trixie's "logic," the girls cleaned off their table, gathered their books, and started to walk to the parking lot, where they were to meet the boys.

Suddenly Trixie stopped and snapped her fingers. "Math problems!" she exclaimed.

"I thought we just decided you don't have any," Honey said teasingly.

"Oh, yes, I do," Trixie said. "I have ten algebra problems that I'm supposed to do for homework tonight, and I left the book in my locker. You two go ahead and wait for the boys. I'll run back and get my book and meet you in the parking lot in a minute." Trixie turned and hurried back down the corridor.

Rounding a corner, Trixie saw Nick Roberts. She started to speak, but something in his attitude stopped her. He stood motionless, his face fixed in a frown, staring at the wall.

Following his gaze, Trixie saw that he was looking at one of the bikeathon posters that Mart had put up earlier.

Mysteries • 9

As TRIXIE WATCHED in frozen silence, Nick continued to stare at the poster. Then, in one swift, sudden movement, he reached out and tore the poster off the wall, ripped it in half, and hurled it to the floor. Next he turned and ran off down the hall.

Trixie remained motionless until he was out of sight. It was only then that she realized she'd been holding her breath. She exhaled in a slow whistle of surprise. *What was that all about?* she wondered. *Can Nick really be* that *opposed to the bikeathon?*

Trixie realized that, short of finding Nick and

asking him point-blank why he ripped down the poster, there was no way for her to know why he had acted as he had. *And I certainly have no desire to corner him on it if he's that angry,* she thought as she hurried to her locker. *He looked as though he might tear me in half as he did the poster.*

Trixie got her math book from her locker and hurried back outside to the parking lot. When she got there, Jim and Honey were waiting in the station wagon.

"Brian and Mart have already left in Brian's jalopy, Trixie," Jim told her.

"Somehow Mart seemed to think it made *much* more sense for them to go ahead and give Di a ride home," Honey added, her eyes twinkling. The other Bob-Whites all knew that Mart Belden had a special feeling for Di Lynch, a feeling that Di returned.

"That means you're stuck with us, Trixie. Hop in," Jim said.

As Trixie walked around to the passenger side of the car, Honey got out and held the door so that Trixie could slide across the front seat next to Jim. Honey then took her place next to the door. Trixie's feeling for Jim was well known, too, and Honey liked to do as much as she could to encourage it.

"Why so quiet, Trix?" Jim asked after they'd driven a few blocks.

Trixie started guiltily, realizing that she'd been lost in thoughts about Nick Roberts. She debated briefly about telling Jim and Honey what she'd just seen in the deserted corridor, then decided she wouldn't. *I don't want to risk turning everyone against Nick, and possibly the whole bikeathon idea.* Aloud she said, "I guess I'm tired. You would be, too, Jim, if you'd just finished explaining the bikeathon over and over and over and over again."

"It really was exhausting," Honey agreed. "Sometimes I'd have barely finished telling someone in great detail how the pledge cards work, when someone else would walk up to the table, pick up a pledge card, and say, 'What's this?' It made me want to scream."

"I had a couple of similar experiences with the posters," Jim said. "I'd walk into a store, and someone behind a counter would say, 'Can I help you?' I'd explain all about the posters and the bikeathon, and, when I'd finished, that person would say, 'You'll have to talk to the boss about putting up a poster in the store.' I'd have to find the boss and start all over again. It's tiring, all right."

Trixie nodded absently, her thoughts returning to Nick.

When Jim pulled into the Belden driveway,

Trixie turned to Honey and said, "Honey, why don't you stay for dinner and spend the night? You haven't stayed over for ages!"

Honey hesitated, knowing that slumber parties on school nights were usually frowned upon by both sets of parents.

"Go ahead, Honey," Jim said. "I'll clear it with Miss Trask. I know you girls have a lot to talk about."

Jim's tone was casual, but Trixie knew that he'd had some inkling of the fight between Trixie and Honey and understood their need to have some time alone to talk. "Thanks, Jim," Trixie said sincerely. "Come on, Honey, let's go!"

When the girls walked into Trixie's house, the delicious smell of Mrs. Belden's pot roast was already wafting through the house. Trixie burst into the kitchen with Honey right behind her. "Moms, can Honey stay for dinner and sleep over? Jim is going to ask Miss Trask."

"That sounds fine, dear," Mrs. Belden said. "In fact, with all of you home from school so late, I can use the extra pair of hands to get dinner on the table by the time your father gets here."

"Gleeps, that's right! This is the night that Daddy gets back from his business trip. I can't wait to see him! Honey, let's hurry upstairs and change clothes. We'll be right back, Moms!" Trixie promised as she rushed out of the kitchen.

"Hold on, Trixie," Honey said as she scurried to keep up. "I thought you were tired!"

Trixie giggled. "I guess the smell of Moms's pot roast revived me."

In Trixie's room, the girls changed clothes, with Honey borrowing a pair of Trixie's jeans and a T-shirt. "You know, Trixie, our families aren't so different, after all. At least, we both change clothes before dinner."

"That's right," Trixie agreed. "Only at your house, you have to change *into* a dress, and here you have to change *out* of it!"

"I think I like your way better," Honey confided. The formal dinners at the Wheeler home, with candlelight and Celia Delanoy, the maid, serving the food, were never as much fun as the meals shared by the noisy Belden clan. "Speaking of dressing, Trixie," Honey continued, "I'll have to go home after dinner and pick up a dress to wear to school tomorrow."

"No, you won't, Honey," Trixie told her. "Remember week before last, when you came over here after school and borrowed my clothes and Brian's bike so that we could go for a ride? You left your school dress here, and it's nicely laundered, thanks to Moms, and hanging in my closet."

"Oh, Trixie, I shouldn't have caused her that

extra work. Remind me to thank her for it when we get downstairs," Honey said.

"I'm sure she'll be happy to let you make up for the extra work by helping with dinner," Trixie assured her. "Let's go."

Downstairs, Mrs. Belden handed out assignments to her willing helpers. Honey was put in charge of getting Bobby ready for dinner, to the delight of both girls. Honey was devoted to the rambunctious six-year-old, since she missed having younger brothers and sisters of her own. Trixie was more than happy to give Honey the chore for once.

Just as Honey led the shiny-faced Bobby back downstairs after his cleanup, the front door opened, and Mr. Belden walked in. The family gathered around him, and he bestowed kisses on Mrs. Belden, Trixie, and Bobby and hugs on Brian, Mart, and Honey.

"It's good to be home," he said. "Especially since my nose tells me I'm just in time for one of my wife's most famous delicacies."

"That's right," Trixie said. "It's all ready for the table, too. Sit down, everybody. I'll bring out the food."

When they were all settled at the table and had begun to eat, Bobby looked accusingly at Trixie. "Honey got my face all cleaned up, Trixie," he said. "And she didn't hurt it at all. She didn't make me promise to eat one whole cooked carrot, either."

"Yipes!" Trixie exclaimed. "Cooked carrots! Dad, what do you know about deutsche marks?"

Even though Mr. Belden was used to his daughter's rapid changes of subject, he couldn't help but look confused. "Deutsche marks are German money, Trixie. West German, I should say. They are a very stable type of currency right now, which means that they can be traded for more than their face value in our money. I don't know what they have to do with cooked carrots, however."

Trixie began at the beginning, telling her father about finding the fifty-deutsche-mark note on Old Telegraph Road and giving it to Bobby as a reward for eating "one whole cooked carrot."

"Brian said he'd seen an article about deutsche marks in one of your magazines, Daddy," Trixie said. "Do you remember what it said?"

Mr. Belden had listened intently to Trixie's explanation, and now he replied, "Indeed I do remember, Trixie. I'd like to see that bank note, if I may."

"I'll show it to you, Daddy. It's in my collection." Bobby jumped up from the table and ran to his room.

Mr. Belden lowered his voice so that Bobby

couldn't overhear. "The article was about counterfeiting, Trixie. Because West German money is so valuable right now, it's become very popular with counterfeiters. They forge large bank notes, like the fifty-deutsche-mark, mix it with some real notes of lesser value, then redeem them at banks for United States currency. Because the banks exchange so much currency every day from people returning from Europe, they seldom think to examine the money. The article was written to inform bankers of the problem and to let us know how we can spot the phony bank notes."

"Here it is, Daddy," Bobby said, returning to the table. "Isn't it beautiful? It's my most favoritest part of my collection."

Mr. Belden took the note from Bobby and examined it carefully for a moment. "It certainly is pretty, Bobby." He passed the note to Trixie. "Look at it closely. Do you see the gray stripe that runs down the left side of the bill? On the real thing, that's made of platinum. It's put right into the paper to make it difficult to duplicate. On this bill, the line is simply printed onto the bill with gray ink. But since this kind of paper can be printed on only one side at a time, it's hard to get the lines to hit exactly the same place on both sides. If you hold the bill up to the light, you can see that the lines aren't in quite the same spot."

By this time, Brian, Mart, and Honey were all clustered around Trixie, looking over her shoulder at the bill. When Trixie held it up to the light, they all saw the shadow of the second line showing through from the other side.

"Gleeps!" Trixie exclaimed. "Then that means that this bill is phony!"

"That's right," Peter Belden agreed. "I think that also explains why it's charred. The counterfeiters realized that this bill couldn't be passed off as the real thing, so they tried to burn it— probably along with a whole batch of poorly printed bills. This one somehow didn't burn completely."

"Let's call the police!" Trixie said, jumping up from her chair so abruptly that she almost collided with Mart, who was still standing behind her.

"The police will certainly have to be notified," Mrs. Belden said. "Brian can drive you to the police station tomorrow morning before school. Right now, we have dishes and homework to worry about, in that order."

"Oh, Moms," Trixie moaned. She didn't continue her protest, however, because her mother was wearing the "no nonsense" look that meant further discussion would not be permitted. *Okay, I'll wait until tomorrow*, she thought, *but don't blame me if I simply explode from excitement before then!*

Back in Trixie's room after dishes and homework

were finished, Honey tried to distract Trixie by talking about the bikeathon. "I think it's going to be a big success, don't you, Trixie?"

"Oh, I'm sure it is, Honey," Trixie replied. "I had thought we might have to set up the sign-up booth several times to get enough people, but everyone was so enthusiastic about it today. I think the kids at Sleepyside are just terrific, don't you?"

To Trixie's surprise, her friend suddenly burst into tears. "Not all the kids are terrific, Trixie. Some of them are just horrid, and you know who I mean. When Ben and his friends started saying those awful things, I just wanted to crawl into a hole and disappear.

"I'm really frightened, Trixie. I've tried to deny it, but Ben has changed a lot. He used to be just a practical joker, but now— Now he seems so hard and cruel. I know he's going to wind up in some kind of terrible trouble.

"It's all my fault, Trixie. I try to be nice to him and spend time with him, but I know he can tell that I don't approve of him, and that just makes him worse." Honey's voice broke, and she covered her face with her hands and sobbed.

"It isn't your fault, Honey," Trixie assured her. "If anyone could turn Ben Riker around, it's you, with all your sympathy and tact. Some people just don't want any help. Nick Roberts is like that, too."

For the first time, Trixie confided to Honey all the details of Nick's strange behavior, from refusing to do the posters to tearing one off the wall at school. She also told Honey what she'd learned from Mr. Crider about Nick's unhappy background. "I'm trying to be patient with him because of that, just as you're trying to be patient with Ben. Still, I can't help but feel that all the sympathy I have for Nick, which is what got me involved in the whole bikeathon idea in the first place, is being wasted on someone who doesn't appreciate it."

Hearing Trixie's troubles had made Honey forget her own, and now it was she who tried to reassure her friend. "You shouldn't feel that it's all a waste, Trixie. The bikeathon is for everyone in the art department, not just Nick Roberts. Think about how grateful Amy Morrisey will feel if we raise enough money for another pottery wheel, so that she can get the practice she needs to become a really good potter."

"I know you're right, Honey," Trixie admitted. "It's just so hard not to feel depressed about it. Here I am, supposedly an expert at solving mysteries. Right now I'm surrounded by people acting in mysterious ways, and I can't begin to figure any of them out."

"Who's acting mysteriously besides Nick and Ben?" Honey asked.

113

"Well, there's Mart, for one. You know how quarrelsome he usually is. But the other night, when I was so upset about our fight, he was nice as can be. He hasn't even teased me about it since you and I made up. That isn't like him at all.

"For that matter, what about me? Don't you think it's pretty mysterious for me to go off and leave the clubhouse window open and all the art supplies out, and then not even to be able to remember doing it?"

Honey gave Trixie a hug as she replied. "Those things aren't very mysterious. Mart's devoted to you, although he tries not to show it. It's perfectly natural that he'd be sympathetic when he knew you were really hurt. And we already figured out that you left the mess in the clubhouse because you were so upset about our fight."

"Oh, I was, Honey," Trixie said. "Even if I never figure out Nick Roberts and Ben Riker, I won't be half as upset as I was when I didn't know if you and I would ever be friends again. Let's never, ever have another fight!"

Honey giggled. "After all your talk about how hard people are to figure out, you should know that it's hard to guarantee that we'll never, ever fight again. I will promise that I'll at least try not to get angry. Although," she added, "if I don't get some sleep, I'll be as grouchy as a bear tomorrow morning. There's only one way to prevent that. Good night, Trixie."

"Good night, Honey," Trixie said, switching off the light.

As she drifted off to sleep, Trixie thought again about the counterfeit deutsche mark and the visit she would make to the police station the next morning. She couldn't help but wonder if she was on the brink of another mystery—one that might be easier to solve than the mysterious behavior of Nick Roberts and Ben Riker.

Suspicious Coincidences • 10

In school the next morning, Trixie thought back to her disappointing interview with Sergeant Molinson.

The sergeant had confirmed her father's opinion that the bill was a counterfeit. He had thanked her for bringing it in and complimented her on her "eagle eye" for having seen the bill against the hedge.

But when Trixie had asked him eagerly if that meant the forgers were operating out of Sleepyside, Sergeant Molinson had responded with a stern warning against getting involved.

"Forgery is a federal offense, Trixie," he'd said.

"That means that the people involved may be desperate—far too dangerous for an amateur detective to get involved with, no matter how much success she's had in the past.

"Besides, finding the bill on Old Telegraph Road isn't much of a lead as to where it came from. The spring winds in this part of the country could blow a piece of paper like that for miles. Or it could have blown off a truck that the forgers were using to take a whole batch of money somewhere to dispose of it.

"At any rate, I'll see that the proper officials are notified, and that they know who turned in the bill. You'll probably get a nice letter of thanks when the case is solved, and I want that to be the end of your part in this."

Then he gave me that stern look of his, Trixie remembered. *I guess that's that. Someone else will have to track down the forgers, while I worry about the bikeathon and my math homework.*

At the end of the day, Di, Honey, and Trixie left the school building together. As they walked, Trixie filled Di in on the discovery of the counterfeit deutsche mark and her meeting with Sergeant Molinson.

"He's right, you know, Trixie," Di said. "Those people could spend a long time in jail if they get caught. I wouldn't want to be the one who catches them. Although," she added, "right now I think I'd rather face a gang of counterfeiters than visit my dentist, which is what I have to do. The toothache that kept me home from school on Monday still isn't much better, so my mother made an appointment for me."

"Then that's why you weren't on the bus this morning," Honey guessed. "You got a ride into town."

"Not exactly," Di said. "Actually, I rode my bike. It was such a nice morning, and I felt it was only right that I, as one of the leaders of the bikeathon, should be practicing what I'm preaching."

"We should all do that," Trixie said. "Only I never make it to the bus stop in the morning with more than a few seconds to spare. I couldn't possibly get ready early enough to ride my bike."

"Speaking of the school bus," Honey said, "here it comes. We'll have to run to catch it. Good luck at the dentist's, Di!"

When they'd settled into their seats on the bus, Honey and Trixie resumed their constant topic of conversation: the bikeathon.

"It's a week from the day after tomorrow, Honey," Trixie said. "That's not much time."

Honey giggled at her friend's unusual way of expressing the date. "Just think, on Monday it'll be a week from the day before yesterday! But

118

you're right. That isn't much time. I think you and I should go to the clubhouse tonight after dinner and make sure we have enough direction arrows. There are quite a few, but we should count them and then review the route in our minds to see how many we'll need."

"Good idea, Honey. We have to make sure that nobody gets lost. Think how upset the riders would be if they missed out on Mr. Maypenny's hunter's stew. Gleeps! Here's your stop already! I'll see you at the clubhouse tonight."

At dinner, Trixie told her parents what had happened at the police station that morning.

"You should have witnessed the crestfallen countenance with which Trixie received our constabulary's warnings that she's to keep her snub nose out of the investigatory scene," Mart chortled. "Please pass the candied sweet potatoes."

"I hope you'll listen to the sergeant's warning this time, Trixie," Mr. Belden said. "He's not trying to spoil your fun, you know. He's genuinely concerned that you'll get hurt someday in the course of your detective work."

"Oh, I know that," Trixie told her father. "It's just that he never even tries to let me know what's going on. I'll have to read about the solution to the counterfeiting case in the *Sleepyside Sun* along with everyone else."

"I'm sure he'd be willing to tell you more," Brian said, "if we all hadn't given him reason to think we'd take the information and use it to get ourselves involved up to our eyebrows in another mystery. Anyway, I'm more than content to let the police handle this one. It sounds pretty dangerous to me."

"I'd be 'tent if I got my s'prise back, Trixie," Bobby said unhappily. "Is Sergeant Molinson gonna keep my s'prise forever?"

"I'm afraid so, Bobby. It was very nice of you to let me take your surprise in to the police, though. He told me especially to say thank you."

"Did he really, Trixie?" Bobby said, his eyes shining. "That means I holped solve a mystery, doesn't it?"

"Oh, no," Mart groaned. "It would appear that the Beldens have another would-be sleuth in their midst. What's to become of us!"

Everyone laughed at Mart's mock despair, and the rest of the dinner conversation turned to other topics, such as what would be planted in the Belden garden that spring.

At the clubhouse that evening, Trixie was happily surprised when she saw how many arrows had already been completed.

"You must have worked like a trooper the other night, Honey. There are more than twenty arrows here! We shouldn't need any more than that."

"Why, Trixie, most of those posters are the ones you did. Even after I threw away the one the paint spilled on, there was still a whole stack of them left. I didn't count exactly, but I'm sure it was more than half of the total."

Trixie shook her head. "I was really in a daze that day, I guess. I'd have sworn that I didn't finish more than five or six posters. I don't remember doing that many, anyway, any more than I remember leaving the window open or the top off the paint jar."

Trixie and Honey were still pondering the surplus of posters when the clubhouse door opened and Di Lynch walked in.

"Well, hi," Trixie said. "You're just in time. We—" Trixie stopped short as she noticed Di's worried expression. "What's wrong?" she asked.

"I tried to call both of you, but Jim and Mart, who answered your phones, said you'd come down here to work. I had the most awful thing happen this afternoon."

"What was it?" Trixie demanded.

Honey looked at Di's pale face and pulled out a chair. "Here, Di, sit down. You look as if you're about to fall over."

"Thanks, Honey," Di said, sitting down at the worktable. "First of all, the trip to the dentist was just dreadful. I had a cavity that felt as though it went clear through to the top of my head, so I was already pretty upset when I left the dentist's office. I was thinking about how good it would feel to take my time and have a nice, calm ride home."

"But what happened?" Trixie repeated, bursting with impatience.

"When I got out to my bike, I discovered that both tires were slashed—that's what happened!" Di wailed. "My brand-new bike!"

"They were both flat, you mean. You probably forgot to put the caps back on the valves, and—"

"No, Trixie, they were slashed! Absolutely cut to ribbons! I just stood there, with my face still numb from the Novocain, staring at my brand-new bike with those totally ruined tires, and I thought, 'Why would somebody do a thing like this to me?' It was just awful!"

"Vandals!" Trixie muttered. "Things like that never used to happen in Sleepyside."

"How did you get home, Di?" Honey asked. "Did you have to call your parents to come and get you?"

"No," Di said. "That's the only lucky part about the whole thing. I had finally decided that that's what I'd have to do, and I knew they'd be upset, because they hadn't really wanted me to ride my bike to town today, anyway.

"But just as I was looking in my purse for a dime

to make the call, Ben Riker drove up and asked me if I needed a ride. I told him what had happened, and he loaded my bike into his car—that is, Mr. Wheeler's car, which he was driving—and took me home.

"Wasn't that a lucky coincidence?" Di concluded with relief.

"I wonder," Honey said quietly.

Trixie and Di both turned to her in surprise.

"Why, Honey, it was certainly lucky for *me*," Di protested. "Otherwise, I don't know how—"

"I wasn't wondering if it was lucky, Di," Honey said. "I was wondering if it *was* a coincidence."

As both girls stared at her blankly, Honey moaned, "Oh, don't you see? What if those friends of Ben's were the ones who slashed your tires? That's just the sort of stupid prank that they might think was fun. What if Ben went along with it, then had second thoughts—or maybe felt bad because he knew it was Di's bike—and came back with his car, waited down the block until he saw Di walk out of the dentist's office, then drove up and offered her a ride, pretending that he knew nothing about what had happened?"

"I see what you mean," Trixie mused.

"Oh, Honey, don't be silly," Di protested. "Ben wouldn't do a thing like that. I'm sure it was pure coincidence, just as Nick Roberts said."

"Nick Roberts? What does he have to do with this?" Trixie asked sharply.

"Oh, I guess I forgot to mention that," Di said. "Nick was standing next to the bike rack when I came out of the dentist's office. He said he'd been walking past on his way home and noticed the slashed tires. He was standing there wondering who the bike belonged to when I walked up."

"I guess that takes the suspicion away from Ben," Trixie said. She told Di about seeing Nick rip up the bikeathon poster. "For some reason— and I'm sure I don't know why—Nick Roberts hates the whole idea of the bikeathon, Di. I'm positive that Nick knew perfectly well who that bike belonged to. He has to know that you're one of the leaders of the bikeathon. Whatever strange reasons made him rip up that poster made him slash the tires on your bike. I'm sure of it. You probably almost caught him at it when you came out of the dentist's office."

"It makes sense," Honey admitted. "That is, it makes sense if you can call two senseless acts making sense. I just wish I were as certain as you are that your theory lets Ben off the hook. Ben and his friends were making fun of the bikeathon the other day at the sign-up, remember? They could be out to stop the bikeathon, too."

"Well, I don't think either one of your theories

124

makes sense," Di Lynch announced. "I think you're both being silly, trying to come up with explanations that don't explain anything. Ben Riker and Nick Roberts may both act strange sometimes, but I don't think that either one of them would deliberately do something as awful as slashing my tires. That poster that Nick ripped up was only a piece of paper, after all—not something as expensive as bike tires. And Ben and his friends may talk a lot, but we haven't seen them actually *do* anything awful yet."

"That's true," Trixie had to admit.

"What should we do?" Honey asked.

"I don't think we should do anything," Di said firmly. "If you tell anybody what you suspect, it will just cause hard feelings if word of it gets back to Nick or Ben. I think we should just wait and see what happens."

Honey and Trixie looked at each other for a moment, each wondering whether something worse would happen if they said nothing. Both girls knew, however, that they had no real evidence on which to base their suspicions.

"Di's right, Honey," Trixie said finally. "All we can do is wait and see what happens."

"And hope we were wrong," Honey added gloomily.

At Mrs. Vanderpoel's • 11

ON SATURDAY AFTERNOON, after the Beldens had finished their weekly chores, Jim and Honey came by in the station wagon to pick them up and drive once more along the bike route, to decide where the directional arrows should go.

Di Lynch was on a shopping trip with her mother, and Dan Mangan was helping Mr. Maypenny patrol the game preserve. But the Bob-Whites had all agreed to meet at the clubhouse later that night to finish their plans for the bike-athon.

Honey had brought along a notebook and pencil so that she could record each of the locations they decided upon for the signs.

"I think the easiest way to keep track will be with the odometer readings," Jim suggested.

"What's an odometer reading?" Trixie asked.

"For the information of those Bob-Whites who are not familiar with the mechanics of the automobile, the odometer is the row of numbers above the steering column that indicates mileage," Mart informed her. "What Jim means is that Honey should write down the exact mileage of every point that we decide should have an arrow."

"Right," Jim said. "When we turned onto Glen Road from the Belden driveway, the final digits on the odometer were three-one-six-point-two. Write that down, Honey. All we have to do is write down the other mileage numbers at each place we choose, then drive the same distance between stops when we put up the signs."

"That *is* easier," Honey agreed. "I was thinking I'd have to write an elaborate code, like 'third maple tree from fourth mailbox from corner,' or something."

"I thought we could use woodsman's symbols," Trixie said, "like the ones Jim taught us when we first met him—bent twigs or piles of pebbles that—"

"That we could only see if we got out of the car and walked the full length of the route," Brian concluded. "Your way would be much more romantic,

Trixie, but I think Jim's is more efficient."

"Here's our first spot, gang," Jim said. "Right here where the bikers will leave the school parking lot on Saturday morning." He read the mileage off to Honey, who wrote it down in her notebook.

Jim continued to drive slowly out of town and down Old Telegraph Road, looking for places where arrows would be easily seen by the riders.

"Wasn't it somewhere around here that you found that German deutsche mark, Trixie?" Honey asked.

"Right over there against that hedge," Trixie said, pointing.

"Has Sergeant Molinson told you whether or not they've found the counterfeiters yet, Trixie?" Jim asked.

Trixie wrinkled her nose. "No, he hasn't, which probably means they're still on the loose. I just wish there were something more that I could do. If Sergeant Molinson hadn't taken the bank note away from me, I could show it to people who live around here and ask them if they had seen any others like it. That way—"

"That way you could scare off the counterfeiters, and they'd quietly pack up and move away and set up their operation somewhere else. Let's face it, Trixie. You don't know enough about the international currency market to be able to solve this case.

Neither do the rest of us," Brian said.

"I guess you're right, Brian," Trixie said. "I'd just assumed, since there was nothing about the bank note in the *Sleepyside Sun,* that nobody was working very hard at finding the forgers. It never even occurred to me that Sergeant Molinson could have good reasons for keeping it quiet. I guess I still have a lot to learn about the detective business. But how am I supposed to learn when all I'm ever told is to 'stay out of the way'?"

Honey had continued to copy down the mileage readings that Jim told her while Trixie spoke. Now she looked up from her notebook and turned to face Trixie in the backseat. "I know, Trix," she said, her eyes twinkling. "I bet those forgers are operating out of the abandoned house Daddy bought. I bet that if we pried the plywood off the doors and windows, we'd find big piles of counterfeit money inside."

While everyone else laughed, Trixie shook her head soberly. "I thought about that, Honey. After all, the hedge where I found that bank note is just down the road from that abandoned house. But I looked at that house carefully right before I found the note. It's sealed up tight as a drum. It's just not a good bet."

"Oh, Trixie, I was just kidding," Honey said. "You have no sense of humor about mysteries."

"We're almost to Mrs. Vanderpoel's house," Jim said, changing the subject to prevent Trixie's being teased about her serious concern for mysteries. "Should we stop for a visit?"

"Oh, yes, let's do!" Honey exclaimed. "I haven't seen her in ages."

"Besides," Mart added, "the way the road to her house wanders around in the woods, we'd better find a place for an arrow about every ten feet, or somebody will be sure to get lost."

"Or think they're lost," Brian corrected. "It's almost impossible to get really lost, since this is the only road, even though it does seem to wander aimlessly for a mile."

As if to prove Brian's point, the road took a sharp curve, then another. Jim slowed the car to a snail's pace, concentrating on the road and reading the odometer numbers to Honey after each curve.

Rounding a final turn, the Bob-Whites saw the neat yellow brick house where Mrs. Vanderpoel lived. Jim pulled into the drive and shut off the car motor. As the sound of the motor died, Mrs. Vanderpoel appeared at the front door of the house. "I thought I heard a car coming up the road," she called. "That sound is so rare out here that I can't help but notice it. Come in, come in!"

The Bob-Whites filed into the house, and Jim explained the errand that had brought them to the neighborhood and their decision to stop for a visit.

"I'm so glad you did," Mrs. Vanderpoel told him. "I just finished making a double batch of oatmeal cookies, as it happens. Would you like some?"

"Yummy-yum!" Honey exclaimed. "Would we ever!"

"Mrs. Vanderpoel, I have never had the misfortune to visit you when there were *not* fresh cookies waiting for me. Is this a case of extrasensory perception on your part?" Mart asked, straight-faced.

The old woman chuckled, her blue eyes crinkling and her rosy cheeks growing even rosier. "Now, Mart, don't you go throwing your twenty-five-cent words at me," she said cheerfully. "I don't know a thing about extra-whatever-you-called-it, but I do know about cookies. I love to bake them, and I love to eat them, too." She patted her ample stomach. "What with one thing and another, they never seem to go to waste, so I just keep making them."

"We're glad you do, too, Mrs. Vanderpoel," Trixie said. "Mart just means he appreciates your cookies going to *his* waist."

"Well, then, why don't you all sit down at the dining-room table while I get us all some milk and cookies?" Mrs. Vanderpoel said, bustling off to the kitchen.

"I'll help you," Honey said, following her. Brian,

Mart, Jim, and Trixie all took places around the table. Trixie ran her hand across the gleaming wood. "I love this table. I love all of Mrs. Vanderpoel's furniture, don't you?"

"It's beautiful," Jim agreed, looking around the room. "These things have all been in Mrs. Vanderpoel's family for generations, and none of them seem to be any worse for being used, instead of roped off in a museum somewhere."

"Bless you, no," Mrs. Vanderpoel said, walking in from the kitchen with a huge platter piled with fragrant oatmeal cookies. "This furniture was made in a time when people had big, busy families and no money to replace their furniture whenever the mood struck them. It was made to last and last. That's something those so-called antique experts don't seem to understand." She set the platter firmly on the table, as if to prove her point about the sturdiness of her furniture.

Honey had followed Mrs. Vanderpoel from the kitchen carrying a tray loaded with glasses of milk. She set one glass in front of each of her friends, then took her place at the table.

"Now," Mrs. Vanderpoel said, settling her ample form at the head of the table, "tell me all about how your bikeathon is coming along."

Each of the Bob-Whites looked around the table, waiting for someone else to begin. Each of them saw four pairs of expectant eyes and four jaws working on oatmeal cookies. Simultaneously, all five of the Bob-Whites swallowed their first bite of cookie, and then all five began talking at once.

As everyone burst into laughter, Trixie said, "You can't expect to get much information when you've just fed us these delicious cookies, Mrs. Vanderpoel. But actually, the bikeathon is going wonderfully, so far."

They all took turns telling her about their plans and about the success of the first sign-up.

Mrs. Vanderpoel listened attentively, nodding her approval. "I've always said nothing makes a person feel quite so worthwhile as creating something with his own two hands. That goes for the artwork your friends make in school, as well as for these cookies that I make, and the needlework I do during the winter months. That's why I think the art department should have as much money as it needs, and I'm happy to help."

Impulsively, Trixie got up from the table and went over to Mrs. Vanderpoel and hugged her. "You're the tops, Mrs. V. Not everyone would be willing to serve cookies to a whole yardful of teenagers on a Saturday afternoon. We really appreciate it."

"A toast to Mrs. Vanderpoel," Mart said, raising his glass of milk.

"To Mrs. Vanderpoel," the Bob-Whites chorused, raising their glasses.

The old woman's eyes glistened, but she replied brusquely. "Oh, piffle! A few cookies and an hour or so of my time aren't worth very much. I'm glad to help. Speaking of cookies, I was going to wrap some up for you to take to your friends Diana Lynch and Dan Mangan, and to little Bobby. I'd best do that right now." She got up abruptly and bustled off to the kitchen.

"I'm afraid we embarrassed her," Honey whispered nervously.

Jim shook his head. "She's pleased, Honey. I could tell. She's just very touched because we showed her that we appreciate her. I'm glad we did."

"Me, too," Trixie said under her breath.

"Here we are," Mrs. Vanderpoel said cheerfully, coming back to the dining room with a plate on which there was another huge mound of cookies covered with foil. "Do you think these will be enough?"

"That's more than generous, Mrs. Vanderpoel," Brian said, standing and taking the plate. "Thank you, in advance, from Dan and Di and Bobby. I'm afraid we have to be going now. We're supposed to meet Di and Dan at the clubhouse."

"We'll see you on Saturday," Trixie said as the

Bob-Whites walked to the door.

"We'll be sure to return your plate then," Mart added. "Good-bye."

"I'll be here waiting for all of you," Mrs. Vanderpoel said. "Good-bye!"

Di and Dan were already at the clubhouse when the others returned. Jim dropped Honey, Mart, and Brian off. "I'll take the car back to the house. I can get some milk to go with the cookies, too. Trix will ride along," Jim said.

Trixie looked at him in surprise but said nothing. Honey winked at Trixie as she got out of the car.

As they walked back to the clubhouse, Jim said, "I haven't had a chance to talk to you alone, and I just wanted to tell you how glad I am that you and Honey have patched up your differences."

Once again Trixie looked at him in surprise. "How did you know—" she began.

"Oh, Honey didn't tell me that you two had had a fight," Jim said. "Although," he chuckled, "I had a feeling that something was bothering her. Especially after she yelled 'touchdown' at the baseball game.

"Seriously, though, Trixie, I knew something was wrong, and I have a feeling that Ben Riker was at the heart of it." Jim sighed. "I can't take sides, because the Wheelers are my family now, and I'm grateful to them for all they've done for me. But

135

I don't approve of the way Ben acts, and I sympathize with you for having to put up with him."

Jim stopped walking and turned to look directly at Trixie. "Anyway, I'm glad that you and Honey made up. I hope you won't let Ben upset you any more. I don't want anything to come between the Beldens and the Wheelers—not ever."

"I—I don't want that, either, Jim," Trixie faltered. "I didn't really realize until the other day at the sign-up how much Honey is being hurt by Ben's behavior and our disapproval of it. It's easier, now, for me to be tolerant. But I'm glad you understand how I feel. It—it means a lot to me."

Jim nodded sympathetically. "I know you pretty well, Trixie Belden—and I like what I know about you," he said. "Let's get this milk back to the clubhouse while there are still cookies left to drink it with."

Too happy to speak, Trixie only nodded.

Back at the clubhouse, Trixie sat in a corner, watching and listening to the banter among her closest friends. *I can't imagine any of us being happier than we are right now,* she thought.

After a while, Trixie's reflective mood passed, and she joined in the chatter. The Bob-Whites discussed the plans for the bikeathon and their hopes for its success. Then the topic shifted to the upcoming end of school and the beginning of summer.

"I can't wait," Di Lynch said happily. "Just think —swimming, lying in the sun—"

"And weeding the garden," Mart groaned, clutching his back as if he could already feel it ache after bending over a hoe.

"We've had one good omen for the summer already," Brian said.

"What's that?" Honey asked.

"Well, it's been quite a while now since Trixie got us involved in a mystery. That just might mean that she's outgrown the phase, and we can spend the summer enjoying ourselves, instead of keeping her out of trouble."

Mart, Dan, and Di laughed, but Trixie and Honey exchanged guilty glances, knowing that their suspicions about Ben and Nick amounted to two more mysteries to solve, even though they'd been telling each other that there was no such thing.

I'd be working on the bank note mystery, too, Trixie thought, *if I knew where to begin.*

As her eyes shifted from Honey's, Trixie saw Jim looking at her, his green eyes trying to read her thoughts.

The Trophy Shop • 12

BY MONDAY, Trixie was feeling restless and distracted. During class, during homework and chores for her mother, Trixie's thoughts continually returned to the bikeathon. She was eager for it to start, and just as eager for it to be over with, so she'd know how much money had been raised.

There was very little she could do, however. At the clubhouse on Saturday, it had been decided that Trixie, Jim, and Brian would man the first rest stop at the deserted house, checking off riders' names and handling the refreshments. Di and Mart were to be at Mrs. Vanderpoel's, and Dan and Honey would help Mr. Maypenny.

When the last riders left each point, the Bob-Whites working there would go to Maypenny's so that they'd all be there for the picnic.

Between now and then, there's just nothing left to do, Trixie thought, *except to hand out pledge cards to people who ask me for them at school and set up the booth on Wednesday to collect the cards.*

When Trixie wasn't thinking about the bike-athon, she was thinking about the counterfeit bank note, wondering what was being done to solve the case. She racked her brain trying to think of something she could do, some way to find a lead, but she had to admit that it was impossible. The closest she came to being in on the case was when her father came home and told the family that the police had questioned the employees at the bank, asking if anyone had tried to redeem any German bills there. No one had.

Brian had errands to run for his mother after school on Monday, and Trixie took advantage of the opportunity to stay downtown and do some window-shopping, hoping that it would provide her with some distractions.

"I'll meet you back here in an hour," Brian told her after he'd guided the jalopy into a parking space on the town's wide main street. "Try not to spend all your money. You have to leave some for your Bob-White dues."

"I've already paid my Bob-White dues," Trixie told him, "as well as a fine for having a button missing from my club jacket at the last meeting. That means I have no money left to spend."

Honey had made all of the Bob-Whites' jackets right after the club was formed. She had worked on them with loving care, fitting the red cloth perfectly and embroidering B.W.G. on the back of each. The Bob-Whites were all very proud of the jackets, and they had decided that any member who appeared in public with his or her jacket in less than top-notch condition would have to pay a fine of ten cents a day to the club treasury. Honey and Di, who always took care to be well groomed, rarely had to pay the fine. Mart, with his love of food, was frequently caught with some remnants of his last meal or snack on his jacket. Trixie, who hated any kind of sewing chore, seemed always to be caught with a torn seam or a missing button. Jim, Brian, and Dan were less concerned with keeping their jackets clean and in good repair than they were with outgrowing them. Honey had already let the sleeves down as far as she could on all three of their jackets, and she'd told Trixie secretly that new jackets might well be good Christmas presents for the boys.

Trixie chuckled to herself as she walked down the street, thinking of Jim, Brian, and Dan all frequently tugging the sleeves of their jackets down over their wrists. *Their sleeves don't seem to stay down much longer than the buttons stay on my jacket when I replace them,* Trixie thought. She wished she had Honey's love for sewing. But Trixie couldn't even master simple things like buttons, much less the kind of beautiful needlework that Honey could do.

Just then Trixie passed the yard goods store, and she stopped for a moment to look through the window at the bolts of brightly colored spring fabric that had just come in. It was all so beautiful, and Trixie thought about the beautiful spring and summer clothing that Honey could make from it. *I'd just go wild if I had to sit still long enough to sew even the simplest skirt. Besides, the beautiful things Honey sews look wonderful on her, but all of my things get wrinkled or stained the minute I put them on. I guess that's why they call me "Tomboy Trixie."*

Walking a little farther down the street, Trixie came to the sporting goods store. Here she lingered for quite a while, looking longingly at the tents and sleeping bags, the shiny ten-speed bikes, and the well-stocked shelves of camping supplies. The Bob-Whites all loved camping out, especially since Jim had taught them so much about woodcraft and the outdoors. Most of their equipment was worn or makeshift, though, since their strict rules about making their own way prevented taking the expensive gifts that Mr. Wheeler would have been happy to give them. The Bob-Whites always hoped that there would be enough money in the treasury for some of the new equipment they wanted, but whenever they had managed to put something aside, they had found some good cause to donate it to.

Trixie sighed deeply and continued on her walk. *This doesn't seem to be cheering me up very much,* she thought, *although it certainly is distracting.*

Soon Trixie had walked past the section of town where the nicer, busier stores were located and was in an area where the shops were smaller and not as clean or well decorated.

She looked into store windows where the displays featured plumbing fixtures and used appliances. In one window, a huge leather shoe, at least two feet long, drew attention to the shoe repair shop inside. Trixie smiled as she looked at it. *Imagine trying to find the owner of a shoe like that!* she thought. *It would be like the story of Cinderella, only in reverse: Whose foot is big enough to fit inside this shoe?*

In the next window, Trixie saw an elaborate display of trophies and ribbons. Some of the trophies were for special activities and had bowlers, baseball players, or even cats and dogs perched on the tops. Others were plain loving cups that could be given out for any special honor. There were also huge ribbons in many colors, some with fancy rosettes on the top. Trixie stared at them, imagining the speeches that would be made as they were presented to their winners and the speeches the winners would make as they accepted the awards.

I wonder how much they cost, Trixie thought. *It would be nice to be able to give something to the riders who finish the whole bikeathon route, or at least to those who earn the most money in pledges. There's only one way to find out.* Trixie opened the door and walked in.

The store looked deserted when Trixie walked in, but a small bell hanging above the door tinkled to tell the owner that someone was in the shop.

For a few moments, no one appeared, and Trixie amused herself by looking at other trophies on display inside the store and at newspaper photographs of people presenting awards to other people.

At last a man emerged from the back of the shop. Trixie saw a look of disappointment cross his face when he saw her standing in his shop alone, and she realized that he did not consider her a serious customer. *And he's probably right,* she thought. *There's not much money in the Bob-White treasury*

143

right now, in spite of all Mart's and my fines.

"Can I help you?" he asked, his tone more polite than hopeful.

"I'm not sure," Trixie confessed. "I just happened to be passing by your window, and it occurred to me that it might be nice to buy some trophies or ribbons for an event that I'm helping to organize. Are they very expensive?"

The man frowned slightly, and his already stooped shoulders sagged a little more. He looked sad and overworked, and Trixie could imagine the feeling of anticipation he'd had when he'd heard the door open and the hopelessness that had taken its place when he'd walked out here to find only a fourteen-year-old girl with sandy hair and freckles, wanting to buy some inexpensive ribbons.

"That depends on what you mean by expensive," the man replied. He walked over to a glass display case in a far corner of the room and pulled out a plain ribbon with the words "First Place" printed on it. "This is the least expensive award I have. It has a card on the back where you can write the date, the name of your organization, and the reason for the award. We carry ribbons for first through fourth place, and they're fifty cents apiece."

Trixie listened carefully, nodding. She started to calculate how much it would cost for four ribbons, and how much that would leave in the Bob-

Trixie took off her jacket and tossed it to Mart. "Thanks for offering to hang up my jacket," she said. "I'm going to go change into my jeans, Moms, and then I'll be right down to help."

Mrs. Belden was taking a casserole from the oven. "Everything's just about ready, Trixie," she said. "Call Dad and the boys when you come back downstairs."

While they ate, Trixie told about visiting the police station. "I told Sergeant Molinson about that helicopter we saw. He said he'd get to work and investigate it immediately."

"I can't imagine why you didn't think of it before this," Mrs. Belden said. "It certainly does sound suspicious."

"We'll see if they mention it on the news after dinner," Mr. Belden said.

Trixie and her brothers hurried to clean up the dishes after dinner and entered the living room just in time to hear the end of the local weather forecast on WSTH.

"And now for more news," the announcer said. "Today, for the first time since the theft of the weather vane from Sleepyside's Town Hall, the police department received what sounded like a promising new lead. Young people reported seeing a helicopter

145

hovering over the Town Hall the week before the weather vane was stolen."

Trixie held her breath and listened intently to the newscast.

"However," the newscaster continued, "the helicopter seen that night was found to belong to the National Guard Training Camp. Student pilots were being trained in night flying. There are still no clues to the whereabouts of Sleepyside's missing weather vane."

Mr. Belden snapped off the radio, and Trixie sagged with disappointment.

"So much for that idea," Brian said. "Too bad, Trix. I thought your idea about the helicopter sounded pretty good."

"Don't worry, Trixie," Bobby tried to comfort her. "You and Honey are real good 'tectives. You'll find Hoppy."

Trixie shook her head. "Maybe. If we're lucky," she said in a dismal voice.

"Here, Trixie," Bobby said. "You can have this." He handed her a rusty metal button. "It's a new good-luck piece I found today."

Trixie smiled. "Thanks, Bobby," she said. Tucking the button into her pocket, she headed upstairs to do her homework.

As she tried to work a math problem, Trixie's mind buzzed with questions. *If they didn't use a helicopter, how did they get Hoppy off that roof?* she wondered. *Maybe they* did *use a giant gorilla!*

A Shocking Discovery • 14

WHEN THE BOB-WHITES entered Sleepyside Junior-Senior High the next morning, they saw a commotion in the hallway outside the social studies classroom. Students and teachers were crowded around the doorway, which was blocked by a burly policeman.

"Jeepers! What's going on?" Trixie wondered aloud.

"I hope no one is sick or hurt," Honey said.

"Let's go find out," Trixie urged, heading for Miss

Craven's classroom. The others were right behind her.

The police officer held them back at the doorway. "No one is allowed in this room at the moment," he said.

"There's Trixie," Miss Lawler said from inside the room. "She and Honey drew the pictures I told you about."

Sergeant Molinson called to the officer at the door. "Let Trixie and her friends come in."

The policeman stepped aside.

As soon as the Bob-Whites stepped into the room, they saw Mr. Quinn's display case tipped over on the floor. The glass had been smashed, and the case was empty.

"The coin collection is gone!" Trixie gasped.

Miss Lawler, chalk-white and trembling, sat at her desk. Miss Craven, distraught-looking and dabbing at her eyes with a handkerchief, nodded to Trixie.

"It's a terrible, terrible thing," Miss Craven said sadly. "I never thought anything like this could happen in our school. I saw a light in this room last night as I drove past, and I'll never forgive myself for not stopping to investigate."

Trixie's eyes met Honey's. Both knew they were sharing the same thought.

Sergeant Molinson opened his notebook. "What time did you drive past the school and see the light, Miss Craven?"

Trixie stiffened, dreading the answer.

"I'm not sure, exactly," Miss Craven said. "I didn't look at my watch. But I believe it was around four, or perhaps a little after four."

Honey gasped.

"Oh, no," Trixie murmured.

"What's the matter?" Di asked softly.

Trixie cupped a hand around her mouth and whispered, "I'll tell you later."

"Did you see anyone around the building, Miss Craven?" the sergeant asked, making notes in his book.

"No, I didn't," Miss Craven said. "Just the light in the classroom."

Sergeant Molinson nodded and turned to Miss Lawler. "Now, how about you, Miss Lawler?" he asked the teacher's aide. "Can you tell us anything at all?"

"No," Miss Lawler answered without looking up. "I—I stayed for a short while after the class had finished, but—"

"Why did you stay?" Sergeant Molinson asked quickly.

"Well, I had some papers to gather up," Miss Lawler said.

Trixie frowned. *She doesn't want to get Sammy involved in this*, she thought. *I wonder if he showed up after Honey and I left.*

"I didn't see anyone in the building as I left," Miss Lawler concluded.

"What time was that?" the sergeant asked.

"Just at four o'clock," Miss Lawler answered in a firm voice. "I'm certain of the time, because I—I had an appointment at four."

Sergeant Molinson closed his notebook and turned to Trixie and Honey. "Miss Lawler is going to lend your reports to us so we can make copies of the coins you drew. Mr. Quinn is out of town, but those papers will give us something to go on. I hope your drawings were accurate."

Trixie and Honey nodded.

"That's all, then," the sergeant said. "I'll be in touch," he told Miss Craven.

For the rest of the morning, Trixie found it impossible to concentrate on her classes. She was uptight and bewildered by the mysterious theft of the valuable coins.

When Trixie and Honey entered the social studies

classroom that afternoon, Miss Craven's eyes were still red and swollen.

"Miss Lawler will not talk about the coins this afternoon," Miss Craven said softly. "By now you are all aware that the coin collection was stolen last night. Instead, we'll begin immediately with today's lesson."

At the end of the period, Trixie and Honey waited while the other students left the room. They carried their books up the aisle to Miss Lawler's desk, and Trixie said, "Miss Lawler, we're—"

Before they reached her desk, Miss Lawler picked up her papers and stood. "I don't have time to talk," she said. She turned abruptly and hurried from the room.

Honey looked hurt.

"She's avoiding us," Trixie said softly.

As the Bob-Whites rode home from school, Trixie suggested a special meeting for the following afternoon, when she knew all of them would be able to come. "We've got two mysteries on our hands now," she said. "And Honey and I have a few things we think you all should know about."

After school on Friday, all seven members gathered at the clubhouse. After Jim called the meeting to order, Trixie took over.

"Honey and I saw something the night before last on the way home from town," she said. She went on to tell about seeing Miss Lawler and the stranger from the belfry shaking hands in front of the school building.

"It was around four o'clock," Honey added. "About the time Miss Craven said she saw the lights on in the social studies room. And we know that Miss Lawler planned to stay late—she told us she was going to wait for Sammy."

Trixie nodded slowly. "But I guess she was really waiting for that stranger. It looks like she helped him steal the coins," she said sadly. "They must be partners in crime."

"Oh, no!" Di protested. "I don't believe it! Miss Lawler wouldn't steal the coins!"

"Why didn't you tell this to Sergeant Molinson yesterday?" Jim asked.

"Because he didn't ask me," Trixie said, flushing. "I wanted to talk about it with the rest of you Bob-Whites first."

"Maybe that man is Miss Lawler's boyfriend," Dan suggested.

Trixie shook her head. "They didn't greet each other like friends. It seemed more like a—a business meeting," she said.

153

Mart pointed a quick finger at Trixie. "Was Miss Lawler carrying a package or anything?" he asked sharply.

Trixie stopped to think. "No," she answered. "But she was carrying that big tote bag she always carries."

Jim groaned. "I've seen that bag," he said. "She could carry *ten* coin collections in it."

Unhappy and frustrated, Trixie pushed her hair back from her hot forehead. "It sure looks like Miss Lawler and that stranger are working together. We all know that Miss Lawler is a new-newmis—"

"A numismatist," Mart put in.

"Right," Trixie continued. "She would know if the coins were valuable. She'd know where to sell them, too."

"I'm afraid you may be right," Jim said.

"Are you going to tell Sergeant Molinson?" Di asked.

Trixie sighed. "We'll have to tell him what we saw," she said. "We don't have any real proof that Miss Lawler was involved, thank goodness. I guess Honey and I will have to stop at the station on Monday after school."

When the meeting was over, everyone was gloomy and quiet. There was none of the chatter and laughter that usually followed their get-togethers.

"It doesn't look very good for Miss Lawler," Brian said as he locked the clubhouse door.

"Well," Trixie said as the Bob-Whites started home, "at least Moms will be happy today—I'll be home in time to help with dinner." She brightened and turned to the others. "Why don't all of you come and have dinner with us? It'll cheer us up. Moms is baking beans and brown bread, and our bean pot is *huge*. There'll be plenty for everybody."

Mart's gloom lifted a little. "Yeah—and we can add spheroids of spicy chopped meat encased in delicate skin—"

Trixie giggled. "He means cut-up hot dogs," she explained. "Mart has trouble with little words like that."

"It sounds good anyway," Jim said. "Your mother makes the best baked beans this side of heaven, Trixie. How about it, Honey, shall we accept this dinner invitation?"

"Let's," Honey answered quickly. "Mother and Dad are in New York, and I'm sure Miss Trask won't mind. I'll call her from Trixie's."

"How about you, Di? Dan?" Brian asked.

"Sorry. I'm out," Dan said. "I'm still cutting firewood. Mr. Maypenny can't handle that anymore."

Di looked disappointed. "I promised Mother I'd

help with the twins," she said. "But thanks anyway."

"Maybe next time," Trixie said.

"Don't worry," Brian added. "Mart'll eat extra helpings in your names!"

Surprising News • 15

IN THE BACKYARD at Crabapple Farm, Bobby was playing with Reddy, the Beldens' big Irish setter. Trixie and the others had cut through the orchard, and Brian signaled them to a halt in the shadows where they could watch without being seen.

"Pay 'tention, Reddy," Bobby said. "This is how you roll over." Bobby rolled over in the leaves that covered the lawn. "See? Now you do it. Roll over!"

Reddy wagged his tail and licked Bobby's face.

"No, no! Don't *kiss!* Roll over!" Bobby rolled over once more. "Like that, see?"

Trixie and the others burst out laughing. "Who is training whom?" Mart asked as they all emerged from the shadows.

"Hi, everybody!" Bobby shouted. "I teached Reddy a neat trick. Watch!" He picked up a large stick and threw it with all his might. "Go fetch, Reddy!" he ordered.

The big dog bounded across the yard after the stick. Trixie and Honey exchanged glances—Reddy was not famous for his discipline.

"Pay 'tention," Bobby urged. "Reddy's a smart dog; you'll see."

Reddy came bounding back with the stick in his mouth. He dropped it at Trixie's feet.

"Good boy, Reddy!" Bobby said, patting the dog vigorously.

Brian shook his head. "That wasn't right, Bobby," he said. "Reddy should have brought the stick back to you."

Bobby shrugged. "Why? I don't want it."

This brought more laughter.

Looking at Honey and Jim, Bobby brightened. "Oh, Honey and Jim, are you going to stay for dinner?"

Brian poked Bobby in the ribs, making him squeal

with delight. "You bet they are," he said.

Jim and Honey followed the Belden young people into the kitchen. "We couldn't help it, Mrs. Belden," Jim said in mock apology. "Trixie and the boys forced us to come for dinner."

"Good! We like company," Mrs. Belden said. She was very fond of Honey and Jim and treated them as if they were her own children. "As long as you're here," she suggested, "why not spend the night?"

"That's super, Moms!" Trixie exclaimed. "Honey and I both have dental appointments in the morning. We'll go together."

"And we'll do some work on my car," Brian, already making plans, said to Jim.

Bobby clapped his hands. "Stay! Stay!" he shouted.

Honey laughed. "We thought you'd never ask," she said. "Of course we'll stay."

"Terrific," Trixie said. "Now tell us what we can do to help, Moms."

"Well," Mrs. Belden said, "the boys can bring in some firewood. We'll pop corn after dinner."

"Oh, boy!" Bobby whooped, heading for the living room. "I'll go fix the pillows on the floor right now."

"And, Trixie," Mrs. Belden continued, "we're all out of hot mustard. Would you and Honey go down to Mr. Lytell's for a jar?"

"That's a long walk, Moms," Brian said quickly. "Jim can drive them down in my car, if he can get it started. Mart and I will bring in the wood."

"Thanks, Brian!" Trixie and Honey chorused.

A few minutes later, Jim, Honey, and Trixie were rattling down Glen Road in Brian's old jalopy. "It's not a limousine," Trixie said, "but it's better than walking!"

At Mr. Lytell's small country store, they parked in front and hurried inside. They were the only customers there, and Mr. Lytell was getting ready to close for the day.

"A jar of hot mustard, please," Trixie ordered.

Mr. Lytell placed the mustard on the counter and waited for Trixie to fish coins from her pocket. "Having a big dinner party?" he asked, eyeing Honey and Jim.

"No, just the family," Trixie answered the inquisitive storekeeper. Honey and Jim exchanged amused glances.

"I see that young fella with the yella truck is back in town," Mr. Lytell said as he counted out the change. "I saw you and Honey riding with him the other day."

"I think you're mistaken, sir," Honey said politely. "Sammy is new in Sleepyside."

"Can't tell me that!" Mr. Lytell snapped. "That yella truck was up and down here all summer long, drag racing on the old Louis Road. And that young fella and his roughneck friends were in this place lots of times."

Trixie looked at Honey and Jim and shrugged. "If you say so, Mr. Lytell," she said. She picked up the jar of mustard and opened the door. "Good night, Mr. Lytell. Thanks."

"Do you think it really was Sammy?" Honey asked when they were back in the jalopy.

"I doubt it," Jim said. "Mr. Lytell might have seen that old truck, though. Sammy may have bought it from someone around here."

As Jim started to back out onto the road, Honey warned, "Hold it, Jim; there's a car coming."

"It's coming pretty fast, too," Trixie added. "It looks like a big station wagon."

Jim looked over his shoulder to watch the approaching car. As the big wagon passed the lighted storefront, the young people had a glimpse of the driver and passenger.

"I think that's Miss Lawler and Sammy!" Honey exclaimed.

"And Miss Lawler was driving," Trixie observed. "She said she couldn't drive!"

"Miss Lawler looked like she was scared," Honey pointed out.

Jim turned onto the road. "Sammy's probably teaching her to drive," he said. "Glen Road is good for beginners—you don't meet many other cars here. Everybody's a little scared when they first start driving. You and Trixie'll find that out."

They were almost home when another car came down Glen Road toward them. "Gleeps," Trixie said. "Glen Road is turning into a regular freeway!"

Jim chuckled as the car went by. "Glen Road isn't private, Trix," he said. "Anybody can use it." He signaled and turned into the driveway at Crabapple Farm. "I hope those beans are ready."

Everyone agreed that the dinner of brown bread, baked beans, and frankfurters was delicious. Mrs. Belden's huge bean pot was scraped clean, and not a crumb of brown bread remained.

When they had finished eating, the young people ordered Mr. and Mrs. Belden out of the kitchen. "Go sit in the living room and relax by the fireplace," Trixie said. "We'll be in as soon as we clean up the dishes."

Trixie and Honey filled the sink with soapy water while the boys cleared the table. Everyone helped dry and put away dishes and silverware.

The boys were already in the living room, and Honey was hanging up her towel, when Bobby came bursting into the kitchen.

"Trixie, I almost forgot," he said. "I found a lot of neat things in the woods today. You and Honey can wash them for me, please." He dropped a fistful of things on the counter. "Thanks!" he added, running back to the living room.

"Here we go again," Honey said with a smile, taking the towel down from the hook.

Trixie spread Bobby's newest possessions out on the counter. "More lucky stones," she groaned. "Two white ones, one black, and one brown this time. And jeepers! Another old baseball card!"

Gingerly, Trixie pushed the muddy card aside, revealing a small round piece of metal under it.

"What's that?" Honey asked, peering over Trixie's shoulder.

"Some kind of coin, I think," Trixie said, picking it up. She washed it quickly and took a closer look. "Honey! This is a Chinese coin! See the writing?"

"Let me see," Honey said, bending to look.

As they studied the coin, Trixie's face paled. "Honey, this might be one of Mr. Quinn's coins! We'd better ask Bobby where he found this."

"Wait, Trixie," Honey said quickly. "We're not *sure* this coin is from the stolen collection. Let's not get everybody excited until we can find out."

"How'll we do that?" Trixie asked. "Mr. Quinn is out of town."

"The library is right across from the medical building," Honey pointed out. "We can stop there after we're done at the dentist."

"You're right," Trixie said, drying off the coin and putting it in her pocket. "I think they have Mr. Quinn's papers on his coin collection. We'll check and see if this coin is mentioned."

They washed Bobby's lucky stones, and Trixie dropped them all into the bottom drawer of the cabinet. "The 'junk drawer,'" she told Honey.

"Don't forget the card," Honey said.

"Ugh. Can't wash that." Trixie grimaced and dropped the dirty card into the drawer with the stones. "Let's go see what everybody else is up to," she urged, heading for the living room.

The Beldens and their guests sprawled on the floor in front of the fireplace, talking and laughing and listening to music on WSTH. Mart convinced his mother to demonstrate her ability with tongue twisters for Jim and Honey, and soon all the young people were convulsed with giggles.

After a while, Mr. Belden brought out the old-fashioned corn popper, and everyone took turns shaking it over the glowing embers. As they munched on the tasty hot popcorn, the music from the radio stopped abruptly.

"We interrupt this program for a word from our news department," the announcer said.

Everyone stopped talking and turned to listen.

"The valuable antique weather vane, thought stolen from the roof of Sleepyside's Town Hall, has been found."

Trixie jumped up. Honey gasped.

"A young man, recently employed as assistant caretaker—"

Trixie said excitedly, "He means Sammy!"

"—discovered the weather vane in a small room directly beneath the belfry of Town Hall. The weather vane, shaped like a grasshopper, was wrapped in canvas and apparently undamaged. Station manager and owner Raymond Perkins will be presenting the assistant caretaker with a check for one thousand dollars tomorrow. We'll have more details on the morning news. Now, back to our music."

"That's impossible!" Trixie exclaimed, jumping to her feet. "I was *in* that room on the day after Hoppy was stolen, and it was completely empty! If Sammy found Hoppy in that room, then somebody had to put him there later."

"Are you absolutely certain the room was empty?" Brian prompted.

"Positive!" Trixie insisted.

"Wow," Mart breathed. "It looks like Hoppy's a phantom weather vane!"

The Stranger Appears Again · 16

TRIXIE WAS OUT OF BED, bending and touching her toes, when Honey opened her eyes the next morning.

"Do you always wake up so full of pep?" Honey asked, yawning.

Trixie laughed. "It's just nervous energy," she said. "I'm excited about Hoppy and nervous about going to the dentist."

Honey giggled.

"I'm going to wear the same jeans I wore yesterday," Trixie said. "They feel good and comfortable now. You'll find clean tops in the second drawer."

The girls dressed quickly and went down to the kitchen for breakfast. Brian, Mart, and Jim were already at the table, helping themselves to scrambled eggs.

Trixie hurried through breakfast, impatient to get downtown. "We have a lot to do this morning," she told the boys.

Jim grinned and looked at Honey. "I guess it's a good thing I went up to Manor House this morning and brought over your bike," he said. "It's outside with Trixie's."

"Thanks, Jim!" Honey said, delighted. "I'm so glad we adopted you," she added.

"Don't forget to brush your denticles," Mart reminded the girls.

A few minutes later, Trixie and Honey were pedaling down Glen Road as fast as they could. They reached town in record time.

The girls stopped at the medical building and put their bikes in the bike rack.

Honey looked over at the common, diagonally

Now I'm sure of it. There's no
bikeathon will put the art dep
ahead than it is now. If there's
that someone could get hurt becau:
isn't worthwhile."

"But—" Trixie began.

Nick ignored her interruption and continued to
talk, his words coming in a rushed, breathless voice.
"How do you think I'd feel—how do you think any
of us in the art department would feel—if we knew
the supplies and equipment we were using were
purchased at the cost of someone's suffering?"

Trixie gulped. That was something she hadn't
thought about.

"Look, Trixie," Nick said, "from what Sergeant
Molinson told me this afternoon, it's obvious that
someone doesn't want the bikeathon to happen. I
think you should call it off. Right away." He
stopped speaking abruptly, as if he'd finally run out
of breath.

He's hiding something, Trixie thought. *He's been
opposed to the bikeathon since long before he
talked to the police. I'm sure that his father is
against it, too. I wish I knew why.*

Aloud, she said, "I appreciate your concern,
Nick. I don't want to see anybody get hurt, any
more than you do. We don't have any real evidence, though, to prove that the vandalism is

ctually connected to the telephone threats. Unless," she added boldly, "you know something more about them."

"I don't know anything about anything," Nick Roberts snapped. "And I don't like your implying that I do. I was just trying to talk sense, but obviously that's impossible to do with you." He hung up abruptly.

Trixie winced as Nick slammed the receiver down. She hung up the phone and turned to find Mart and Brian staring at her.

"That was Nick Roberts," she explained lamely. "He doesn't seem to think the bikeathon is a good idea."

Brian shook his head. "I don't think I do, either, Trixie. I know you have your heart set on helping the art department, and it's hard to abandon the project now, when all the pledge cards are in and we know how successful the bikeathon could be. But I think we have to decide—soon—if the dangers don't outweigh the advantages."

Trixie looked at Mart. "What do you think?" she asked him. "Are you still willing to go ahead with it?"

Mart shrugged. "I don't know what to say. I was almost hoping that Ben Riker or Nick Roberts would turn out to be the culprit, since that would at least solve the mystery and take us off the hook.

Now we know that Ben Riker is innocent, and I guess we can assume that Nick is, too, since Sergeant Molinson let him go after he was questioned.

"That means that whoever made those threats is still at large. And *that* means that there is a certain amount of risk involved with going ahead and having the bikeathon on Saturday.

"I just don't know what to say, Trixie," Mart concluded helplessly.

"I'll tell you what," Trixie said. "Tomorrow morning before school, we'll all get together and have a vote. The majority rules. If at least four of the Bob-Whites vote to cancel the bikeathon, we'll go right to the principal's office and ask him to announce it over the PA. Otherwise, we'll go on as scheduled."

"That seems fair," Brian said. "It also gives us a night to sleep on our decision, which I intend to begin doing immediately. Good night."

Before she fell asleep, Trixie once again turned over in her mind her growing suspicion that the counterfeit bank note she'd found was somehow tied in with the attempts to have the bikeathon canceled. *Ben Riker already is a forger, in a way, because of the arrows. And Nick has enough artistic talent to make a bill like that.*

Suddenly Trixie sat bolt upright in bed. "Mr. Roberts," she murmured into the dark room. "He's an *engraver!* I'm sure I've read that people who draw the pictures on money are called *engravers.*" She thought the idea over, then shook her head. "If Mr. Roberts were a counterfeiter, he wouldn't be working all day in that shabby trophy store. The family wouldn't still have money troubles, either, as Mr. Crider said they did. Still. . . ." Trixie shook her head again to dismiss the thought, then lay back down and drifted off into a troubled sleep.

The next morning, Trixie was both relieved and nervous when all the Bob-Whites boarded the school bus for the ride to town. *We can have the vote right here on the bus,* she thought. *At least it will all be over soon—one way or the other.*

She signaled for the others to join her at the back of the bus, where they could have relative privacy.

With their heads bent close to Trixie's, Di, Dan, Honey, and Jim listened while Trixie told them briefly about the phone conversation she'd had with Nick Roberts the night before, and about the decision that she and her brothers had made to ask the Bob-Whites to vote on whether or not to cancel the bikeathon.

When she had finished, she looked around at the solemn faces of her friends. Then she opened her notebook, took out a sheet of paper, and quickly

172

tore it into seven pieces. Trixie handed the pieces of paper to her friends, saying, "We'll have the voting by secret ballot. Just write 'yes' if you think the bikeathon should go on tomorrow as scheduled, and 'no' if you think it should be canceled."

Trixie quickly wrote "yes" on her own ballot, then folded it in half. Brian and Mart both wrote their votes quickly and handed their folded ballots back to her. She looked at her brothers intently, but she couldn't tell from their expressions which way they had voted.

Jim also made his decision quickly and handed the folded paper to Trixie. Dan, Di, and Honey each thought for several moments before they wrote their votes and, with solemn expressions, handed the last three ballots to Trixie.

Trixie stared at the seven folded pieces of paper in her hand. *This is it,* she thought. *In a minute we'll know whether the bikeathon goes on or not.*

"Hurry up, Trixie," Honey urged. "Count the votes. I can't stand to wait another moment!"

Trixie's hands were shaking as she unfolded the first piece of paper. " 'Yes,' " she read. She unfolded the next piece of paper. " 'Yes.' " Her hopes soared: Maybe the vote would be unanimous for having the bikeathon. Her hopes plummeted when she unfolded the third ballot. " 'No.' "

The fourth ballot was also a "no," and Trixie

173

felt her stomach tighten. Three folded pieces of paper remained, and they would be the deciding ones.

The three remaining votes were all "yes."

"Yippee!" Mart cheered, removing any doubt as to which way *he* had voted. The other Bob-Whites did their best to remain expressionless.

Trixie sighed with relief. The bikeathon would go on as scheduled, she announced.

Then her feeling of relief left her and tension took its place as she realized what the vote meant: The Bob-Whites were once again divided. Two of the club members were opposed to the bikeathon, and, although they would go along with the decision of the majority, the vote wouldn't be enough to remove their fears.

What if something does go wrong? Trixie thought. *What if somebody wants to stop the bikeathon enough to do something desperate, and Sergeant Molinson's men can't stop it from happening? How will the Bob-Whites feel about each other then?*

Trixie scanned her friends' faces as if she hoped to find the answer written there. All she found was six pairs of troubled eyes looking into her own.

At the Abandoned House • 16

THE REST OF the school day passed without incident, although Trixie was nervous and inattentive. She jumped and looked at the door whenever she heard a noise in the hallway, half expecting to be summoned to the principal's office and told of another incident that would mean that the bike-athon must be called off.

As the day wore on, Trixie began to relax. *If something else were going to happen, it would have happened by now*, she thought. *I don't think we have anything to worry about during the bike-athon. The threats were meant to make us cancel it. Whoever made them has probably given up hope*

175

of scaring us into calling it off.

Still, she had to admit that that was only an optimistic guess. Not knowing who had made the threats—or why—she could only keep her fingers crossed until the bikeathon was actually over.

By the time Trixie boarded the school bus that afternoon, she was almost cheerful again. "Just think, Honey," she said, bouncing up and down on the seat in her excitement, "by this time tomorrow, it will all be over. We'll have checked off all the riders who returned to the school parking lot, and we'll know exactly how much money they earned."

"That doesn't mean it's all over," Honey reminded her. "We still have to make all those phone calls to the sponsors, letting them know how much money they should send in."

Trixie dismissed Honey's reminder with a wave of her hand. "There's nothing to that—just a few phone calls apiece if we divide up the cards. I mean the hard part will be over, and the—" Trixie stopped in midsentence, her nervousness returning again.

" 'And the danger,' you were going to say, weren't you?" Honey asked. "I've been thinking all day about that phone call I got, and the phone call Mrs. Vanderpoel got, and Di's tires, and Mr. Maypenny's game cart, and— Oh, Trixie, I hope we did the right thing, deciding to let the bike-athon go on tomorrow. I'm almost sure that Jim voted against it."

"I think Brian did, too. We made the right decision, though. They'll see," Trixie said, trying to keep a confident note in her voice that she didn't really feel. "Here's your stop, Honey. See you tomorrow morning!"

Soon after, Trixie and her brothers got off the bus and began walking up the long driveway to their house. They were several yards from the door when they heard the unmistakable sound of Bobby Belden's most anguished wail. They exchanged worried glances, then ran up the driveway to the kitchen door, which was opened slightly.

"What is it? What's wrong?" Brian asked as he ran up to his mother, who was standing on the back step.

"Bobby's locked himself in the house," Mrs. Belden said, looking harassed. "Apparently he put the chain lock on when I stepped out for a moment, then couldn't remember how to unlock it when I wanted to get in. He didn't realize the front door was already locked. Now he thinks he's trapped, and he's too frightened to listen to my instructions on how to work the lock."

Mart and Trixie walked up to the door. At close range, Bobby's screams were deafening.

"Don't worry, Bobby," Trixie shouted above the noise. "We'll have you out in no time." She looked up at Mart with an expression that said, "But how?"

Mart thought a minute, then cleared his throat and put his head close to the door. "Slide the chain to the far end of the bracket, Bobby," he said loudly through the narrow opening.

Bobby wailed even more loudly. "I don't know what's a bracket, Mart. Get me out! Holp, please, holp!"

Trixie suppressed a grin as she saw the look of exasperation on Mart's face.

"Clear the way," Brian said behind them.

Trixie turned and saw Brian bringing a hacksaw from the garage. "Bobby has already decided he can't understand you," he said. "There's no sense wasting your breath. We'll just have to saw the chain."

While Trixie, Mart, and Mrs. Belden watched anxiously, Brian pushed the hacksaw into the narrow opening between the door and the doorjamb and carefully sawed through the chain.

Bobby ran into his mother's waiting arms the minute the door opened and continued to sob while Brian took the hacksaw back and put it in the garage.

By the time Brian returned to the house, Bobby had stopped crying and was sitting quietly, his breath still coming in hiccuping gasps. "Th-Thanks, Brian," he said. "You saveded my life."

Brian chuckled. "It wasn't quite that drastic," he said. "But, Bobby, why on earth did you decide to lock the door?"

"I don't know," Bobby said sheepishly. "Because I never lockeded it before, I guess."

Seeing Bobby's lower lip begin to tremble again, Trixie fought to keep from laughing. Instead, she put her arms around her little brother and hugged him. "Well," she said, "now you *have* locked it, and you don't ever have to do it anymore, right?"

"Right," Bobby said, nodding emphatically.

At dinner that night, the story of Bobby's adventure was the sole topic of conversation. Now that he felt he was out of danger, Bobby relished telling his father about his own fright and his oldest brother's heroism in rescuing him.

Partly in order to give Bobby something else to think about, Peter Belden suggested that the whole family go to an early movie as soon as dinner was over.

The rest of the family accepted the invitation eagerly, but Trixie asked to be excused. "It would be a waste of your hard-earned money, Daddy," she said regretfully. "All I can think about tonight is the bikeathon tomorrow. You go ahead and bring

179

back a full report. Maybe Honey will want to go with me later if it's a good film."

As soon as her family left, however, Trixie began to regret her decision. *At least the movie might have distracted me for a minute or two,* she thought as she wandered aimlessly through the quiet house. As it was, she had nothing to think about but the bikeathon and whether or not those telephone threats would be carried out.

Or I could think about the ring of counterfeiters, she thought, turning on the television and sprawling on the couch. *Although I'm sure that the two are somehow related. Isn't that silly? I have nothing to base that feeling on but a dumb, scary dream, but I can't seem to shake it, any more than I can shake my suspicions of Ben and Nick.*

Trixie watched the local news, then stared unseeing at a situation comedy that followed. As the program ended, she stood up, stretched, and turned off the set. *I hope the other viewers got more laughs out of that show than I did,* she thought, with a sigh.

Going out to the kitchen for a snack, Trixie's eyes fell on the sawed-through chain. It reminded her of the time the lock on the bathroom door had jammed shut when Mr. Belden was fixing the plumbing, and he had had to pry the hinge pins loose in order to get out.

Trixie opened the refrigerator, then froze, her hand reaching for a carton of milk. "Hinges!" she shouted into the empty house. "That's it! The hinges were on the *outside* of that boarded-up house!"

She turned and ran out the door, tugging on a jacket as she ran. She got her bike out of the garage and pedaled as fast as she could toward Old Telegraph Road.

A few yards from the spot where the driveway of the abandoned house turned off the main road, Trixie got off her bike and walked beside it. She wheeled it quietly up the gravel drive and lowered the kickstand carefully with her foot.

Her eyes straining in the darkness, Trixie made out a shadowy form next to the house. Walking toward the form, Trixie saw that it was a van—and she saw that there was a light coming from the back of the house.

Trixie crouched down next to the van and looked toward the light. In the silence, she heard gruff-sounding men's voices coming from the back of the house.

"This was a sweet setup we had here," one man said. "I still say we should just leave the stuff here."

"No way," another voice replied. "It's too risky now. With fifty kids milling around here tomorrow, somebody could discover that this cellar door has been opened recently. Then our goose would really be cooked."

"The door's locked," the first man said. "If those kids see that big padlock in place, they're not going to notice that we've been taking out the hinge pins and walking right in. Even the guy who comes over to clean up the yard hasn't noticed it. I think it's a lot more dangerous to go driving around the country with a bunch of counterfeit money than it is to—"

Just then, Trixie's bike, which had been parked on the loose, unsteady gravel in the drive, tipped over with a crash.

Trixie hesitated, unsure whether to stay hidden by the van or make a run for it. She hesitated too long. When she finally stood up to make a dash for the road, she succeeded only in stepping into the ray of a flashlight carried by one of the men coming around from the back of the house to investigate the noise.

Trixie turned and started to run, but the dark-haired, burly man quickly overtook her. He seized her by the arm and held it in a viselike grip, dragging her around to the back of the house and shoving her roughly through the open cellar door.

"Look what I found," he called. "It's the leader of those bikeathon kids."

Trixie stumbled down the steep stairs and found

herself face-to-face with the other man. He, too, was dark-haired, but he was less husky than the man who had pushed her. He looked no less menacing for his smaller size.

"You're the one that people call the amateur detective, aren't you?" the smaller man snarled. "We thought we'd have trouble with you before now. That's why we kept away from you with our threats and tire-slashing. Well, you finally got too nosy. Now you're going to have to be loaded into the van with all the other stuff we have to dispose of." He moved menacingly toward her, and the big man grabbed her from behind, stuffed a rag into her mouth to keep her from screaming, and tied her hands together behind her back.

He pushed her into a dark corner of the cellar, saying, "Stay here until we're ready to leave."

Trixie felt the sticky, clinging fingers of a cobweb against her face. She shook her head to free it, and the tears that had been standing in her eyes rolled down her cheeks.

They were going to dispose of her, the man had said. Trixie shuddered as she thought about what that might mean.

Why did I have to come out here by myself? she thought desperately. *Why didn't I wait for Brian and Mart to come back from the movie, or call Jim and Honey?*

She realized that she'd left the house so hurriedly that she hadn't even taken time to write a note. *I thought I'd be back before my family was,* she brooded. More tears rolled down her cheeks as she thought about her family returning from the movie and finding her gone.

They'll start to worry right away, she thought. *They'll call Honey to ask if I'm at the Manor House, and then Honey and Jim will start worrying, too. Someone will discover that my bike is missing, but that won't tell them where I've gone. By the time they do find it, I'll be— Where? In the Hudson River, probably.* Trixie choked down a sob.

The smaller man heard the noise and turned around, his face a cold mask. "Pipe down, kid," he ordered.

Trixie did her best to return his look with an angry one. When he turned his back, she looked away from him to the contents of the room, and what she saw was so surprising that, for a moment, she forgot her fear.

It's a regular printing shop! she thought. In one corner of the room stood an old-fashioned-looking printing press. There were pallets loaded with paper, drums of ink, and boxes filled with the finished product: fifty-deutsche-mark notes, just like the one she had found.

Trixie also noticed a fireplace that was filled with charred pieces of paper. *That's where my note came from,* she thought. *They were burning rejects, and somehow one note blew up through the chimney before it burned completely.*

The smaller man saw Trixie staring and turned to look at the fireplace. "We have to put those ashes in a bag and take them with us," he told the bigger man. "We don't want to leave any clues behind. Otherwise we won't be able to set up shop in this area again." He smiled evilly at Trixie, his eyes glittering. "You tipped me off, kid. Thanks to you, we should be able to make a clean getaway."

Trixie flushed with anger—anger at the cruelty of the little man and anger at herself. *Now you've done it,* she thought. *You've destroyed the one clue that might have made those men get caught.* She tugged at the ropes that bound her wrists, frantically hoping that she might be able to free herself and make a run for the cellar door. The ropes held tight.

Trixie let her body sag against the wall and watched silently as the men continued their moving operations. The smaller man was packing paper, ink, and counterfeit money into boxes, which the big man carried to the van. Then the smaller man began to take apart the press, and his accomplice strained to carry the heavy metal pieces up the stairs.

After what seemed like hours, the cellar was empty. "You take the girl out to the truck," the smaller man said. "I want to take one last look around, to make sure we didn't forget anything."

The big man grunted in agreement, grabbed Trixie by one arm, and dragged her to her feet. He pushed her up the stairs, caught her roughly as she stumbled, and guided her out the door.

When they got to the van, the big man lifted her up, as if she were a sack of flour, and tossed her into the back, closing the doors behind her.

In the darkness, Trixie groped and stumbled, trying to find a place to sit. She settled herself uneasily on a pallet of paper. She heard the big man grunt again as he boosted himself into the vehicle, then heard the door on the driver's side of the van slam shut.

Trixie heard a slight rustling sound and felt a hand on her arm. She tried to scream.

"It's okay, Trixie," Nick Roberts's voice whispered close to her ear. "Don't make any noise. I'll get us out of here." Nick crouched behind a stack of boxes as he heard the smaller man trudge up the cellar steps, slam the door shut, and pound the hinges back into place. He walked around to the passenger side of the van and climbed in.

"Let's go," he barked.

As the motor started, Nick removed Trixie's gag and began to untie her hands. A jumble of thoughts raced through her mind. *What's Nick doing here?* she wondered. *And how is he going to get us out of this van without their knowing about it?*

She heard the grinding sound as the driver put the engine in gear and the groaning noise of the heavily loaded vehicle starting to move forward.

Suddenly the glare of floodlights pierced the darkness, and she heard a familiar voice call, "Stop that van and come out of there. This is the police."

Trixie looked at Nick in astonishment and saw that he looked as surprised as she felt. The van jerked to a stop. Trixie cautiously opened one of the back doors and peeked around its edge. She watched the big man crawl slowly out from behind the wheel, his hands raised over his head.

The other man hesitated a moment, then yanked open the door, jumped to the ground, and started to run across the clearing.

"He's getting away!" screamed Trixie. Heedless of her danger, she clambered out the back of the van and scrambled to the ground, with some confused idea of giving chase to the counterfeiter.

"Are you crazy?" yelled Nick Roberts. "You'll get yourself killed!"

The counterfeiter had almost reached the woods when another figure emerged from the shadows and caught the fleeing man with a flying tackle. "I've got him!" Trixie heard a familiar voice shout. It was Jim Frayne!

Explanations • 17

THE TWO SCUFFLED BRIEFLY, then Sergeant Molinson ran over and pulled the counterfeiter away, leading him to a waiting patrol car, where his accomplice slouched sullenly in the backseat.

After a quick examination of the contents of the van and a few words with Nick Roberts, Sergeant Molinson turned to one of the policemen he had with him. "You drive that load of evidence to the station," he ordered. Just before he drove away in his own car, he called out to Trixie, "I have a few things to say to you later, young lady!"

Jim had stood up and was dusting himself off after the scuffle. "Oh, Jim, are you all right?" Trixie asked anxiously, running up to him.

Jim looked at Trixie and started to reply, then did a double take. "I think that's supposed to be my line, Trixie," he said, laughing. "But since you ask, I'm fine, thank you." His green eyes turned serious. "How are you? That's the more important question."

For the first time, Trixie had a chance to stop and think about how she felt. She was shaking like a leaf, she realized, and there was a lump in her throat that wouldn't go away no matter how hard she swallowed. Overall, though, she couldn't remember ever feeling quite so good. "I—I feel just great, Jim, now that you're here. But how—"

"How did we deduce the whereabouts of our peripatetic sibling?" Mart asked as he, Brian, and Honey walked up behind her. "Elementary, my dear Beatrix."

Trixie jumped as she heard Mart's familiar voice, then gave a happy cry and threw her arms around each Bob-White in turn.

"We got home from the movie to find you missing, and we immediately got worried because it was already after dark," Brian explained. "We called Honey, to find out if you were with her. You weren't, of course, and she began to worry, too. She and Jim came over in the station wagon immediately. By that time, we'd already discovered that your bike was gone."

Trixie nodded guiltily as Brian told the story, which was so much like the one she'd imagined when she was tied up in the cellar of the abandoned house. *I had them all so worried,* she thought. *I feel just awful about that. Thank heavens, in real life they figured out where I was.*

"How did you find me?" she asked aloud.

"I defer to your distinguished colleague," Mart said, bowing low to Honey.

Honey blushed as they all turned their attention on her. "Well, Trixie, your bike was gone, and it's the night before the bikeathon, so it didn't take much detective work to figure out that you were somewhere along the route. Why I thought immediately of this abandoned house, I'm really not sure. I guess it just seemed the most likely spot, since it is abandoned, and since it's the rest stop you'll be at tomorrow morning." Honey gave up trying to explain and simply shrugged. "Maybe it's just because I know you so well, Trixie," she finished.

Trixie hugged her friend gratefully. "I'm glad you do, Honey," she said. "If you hadn't been here, with the police— Who called the police?"

Mart and Brian looked at Honey and Jim, and Honey and Jim looked at Brian and Mart. No one seemed to know. Finally Mart grinned. "I think

Moms will have the answer to that question when we get home," he said. "She and Dad were awfully worried, and Dad took off to look for you along Glen Road. Moms didn't want to let us drive over here, but we insisted that we had to. I guess she figured it couldn't hurt to send us some reinforcements. Sergeant Molinson has probably already called her by now, to tell her we're all out of danger."

"I hope that's why he left so abruptly," Trixie said. "I was afraid he was too angry at me right then even to give me his usual stern lecture about not getting involved in police business."

"I may give it in his place," Jim said, only half teasing. "You almost got yourself into a lot of trouble."

Trixie looked at the ground and nodded. "It would have been even worse if Nick hadn't—Nick!" Realizing that she'd forgotten all about the young art student since the police halted the van, Trixie raised her head and looked around the dimly lit clearing.

Nick was standing just a few yards away, wordlessly listening to and watching the Bob-Whites' reunion. Trixie hurried over to him, grabbed his arm, and practically dragged him back over to where her friends were standing.

"Nick was in the van that those two men had,"

Trixie explained. Seeing her friends' suspicious looks, Trixie realized that they didn't fully understand the reason for Nick's presence at the abandoned house. *I guess I don't either,* she realized, looking at Nick questioningly.

Nick's face became sullen as the Bob-Whites continued to stare at him. "I wasn't in on the counterfeiting scheme, if that's what you're thinking," he muttered.

"Oh, Nick, of course we don't think that," Trixie assured him. "I'm awfully, *awfully* happy that you happened to be here. We're just wondering—well —*how* you happened to be here."

Nick looked around at the others, paused for a moment, and then began to speak. "It all started the day you called me about the bikeathon. Remember that, Trixie?"

Trixie nodded. *How could I forget?* she thought.

"I guess I wasn't very polite when you called," Nick admitted. "I'm not naturally optimistic, anyway, and after the poor turnout we'd had for the art fair, my first thought was that the bikeathon would just be another wasted effort."

Nick was silent for another moment, then cleared his throat. "That wasn't really all of it. I was angry with you because your friend Ben Riker had broken Amy Morrisey's vase, and because I'd read about you in the newspaper, after you helped solve that

193

mystery about the stolen weather vane.

"You all seem to be such insiders, and I've always felt like an outsider since we moved to Sleepyside."

Just like Ben Riker, Trixie thought. *I bet Nick would never believe me if I told him that Ben felt exactly as he does.*

"After I thought about it for a while, I started to see that the bikeathon might not be such a bad idea after all," Nick continued. "Just because you people *are* insiders and know Sleepyside so well, I thought that you might be able to create some enthusiasm for the bikeathon and, as a result, raise some money for the art department.

"By dinner time, I was really getting excited about the bikeathon, and I told my parents everything you'd told me about it—the route it would take, how the pledge cards would work, and so forth.

"My father got very upset about the whole idea," Nick said. "He absolutely refused to let me take part in the bikeathon. When I tried to protest, he got even more upset. He threatened to throw me out of the house if he ever found out that I'd taken part in the project, and he said that I should try to convince you not to have it at all."

Nick's face contorted, as if he could still hear his father's angry words ringing in his ears. He shook his head as if to dispel the sound.

"My father is a very old-fashioned man, in many ways," Nick continued. "In some ways that's good. He has an old-fashioned pride in his work that I've always respected very much. I think that's why I got involved in art—I wanted to do something that I could feel as proud of as he does." Nick looked around him as if begging someone to understand what he was saying. Trixie looked at her friends and saw that their expressions had changed from suspicion to sympathy—sympathy with a touch of admiration.

"In other ways, my father's old-fashioned attitudes are harder to live with. He doesn't like to be questioned by me or my mother. He believes that, in his house, his word is law. I knew that he would carry out his threat to throw me out of the house, and I could see that our argument was upsetting my mother, so I dropped it.

"I knew, too, that my father doesn't believe in taking charity. No matter how broke we've been—and believe me, we've been pretty broke in the past few years—Dad would never ask for outside help. I figured that was why he was so upset about the bikeathon. He thought that would be like taking money from strangers, I decided."

Nick fell silent again. Trixie could see beads of perspiration on his forehead and his upper lip.

She wondered whether Nick was going to tell them that his father was working with the counterfeiters. She wanted to blurt out the question, but she held her tongue. Nick was not usually a very open person, she knew. Even Mr. Crider had said that nobody really knew Nick Roberts. She realized that any interruption in his telling of the story might make him decide not to finish it at all. The other Bob-Whites seemed to sense it, too, because they all waited quietly for Nick to continue.

"I owe you an apology, Trixie," Nick said finally. "I was very rude to you that morning in school when you wanted to talk to me about the posters. I couldn't explain to you what had really happened, and I didn't know what else to do. I'm sorry."

"It's all right, Nick. I understand now," Trixie said, her voice barely above a whisper. For a moment she thought Nick had said all he was going to say, but then he began to speak again.

"When the police questioned me about those telephone calls, I began to suspect that there was more to my father's attitude than just not wanting me to accept charity. I brooded about it for a couple of days, and tonight I finally demanded an explanation.

"Dad told me that some men had come to him a month or two ago. They asked him if he'd like to make a lot of money doing some complicated engraving. He asked them what kind of engraving. One of the men—I think it must have been the little man that the police caught tonight—winked slyly and told him, 'Let's just say you'll be making lots of money.'

"Dad realized they were talking about counterfeiting, and he said he couldn't allow something like that in his shop. 'You wouldn't have to,' the little man said. 'We have our own setup.' Then that big guy, who must be more muscle than brains, volunteered that it was on Old Telegraph Road. Dad said the other man gave the big one a murderous look and ordered him to shut up, and for a moment Dad was afraid he had already learned too much.

"He stuck to his guns, though, and said he wouldn't have anything to do with the scheme. The little man shrugged and said that was fine, but he warned him not to go to the police. 'Your wife will get a whole lot sicker than she already is if you do,' he said.

"Of course, Dad didn't dare tell anybody about the counterfeiters, but when I told him where the bikeathon route would be and that the abandoned house was the first stop, he remembered what the big man had blurted out, and he realized that it might be the same place. That's why he ordered me not to get involved.

"As soon as Dad finished telling me the whole story tonight, I took the car and came out here. I parked down the road and walked up here. The men were loading the van, and so I waited until they were both in the cellar and climbed inside. I thought I could ride along and find out where they took it, then hop out and call the police. Then Trixie came along and—well, I guess you know the rest," Nick finished abruptly, as if his long speech had used up his entire allotment of words.

There was another long silence as everyone thought his own thoughts—about Nick's courage, Trixie's daredevil actions, and the narrow escape the two young people had just had from the desperate and dangerous criminals.

"I think what you did was perfectly wonderful, Nick," Honey said, breaking the silence. "It took a lot of courage to come out here, knowing all along what you were going to find."

Nick shook his head regretfully. "If I'd had real courage, I would have stood up to my father two weeks ago, and this never would have happened."

"You couldn't take chances with your relationship with your family, Nick. We all understand that." Jim's voice was quiet but firmly reassuring. Trixie guessed that Jim was thinking of his own problems with his stepfather, before Jim had run away and had been adopted by Honey's parents.

"Anyway, my delaying put you all through some bad times, with the telephone threats and the tire-slashing and the destruction of Mr. Maypenny's game cart. I heard those two bragging about doing all of those things, while I was hidden in the truck. They weren't the least bit sorry for doing them, either—except that they didn't succeed in getting you to cancel the bikeathon."

"Are you sure those men mentioned doing all of those things?" Brian asked. "If so, the whole mystery is cleared up."

Trixie nodded her affirmation of what Nick had said. "The little man confessed to doing most of those things, while I was in the cellar. I shouldn't say he confessed, though, because he didn't sound a bit sorry, as Nick said."

"I'm the one who's sorry," Nick said. "I almost ruined everything. Is there something I can do to make up for it?"

"I'd say you more than made up for everything tonight," Trixie said, "when you were there to save my neck."

Honey, Jim, and Brian nodded.

"Not quite," Mart said severely. The others looked at him in surprise.

Don't tell me he's still suspicious of Nick, Trixie thought in alarm. *That would drive Nick right back into that shell of his, which he's almost shed.*

Then she saw the twinkle in Mart's eyes, and she felt herself relax.

"There's still the little matter of the bikeathon tomorrow," Mart told Nick. "I'd say the least you could do is to show up tomorrow afternoon and help dish out the hunter's stew to that hungry mob. There might even be a spare bowlful for you. What do you say?"

"I say I'd be delighted to help," Nick said with a smile. "I'm sure I can get time off from work. Just give me directions on how to get there."

As the other Bob-Whites rummaged for a scrap of paper and Jim sketched a map for Nick, Trixie suddenly felt very, very tired. She realized that only her curiosity had been keeping her awake for the past few minutes. Now that it was satisfied, she felt positively bone-weary.

Seeing her yawning broadly, Jim put his arm around her shoulders and led her toward the station wagon. "We'd better get you home, young lady," he said. "You've had a busy day."

He settled her in the car, and she was almost asleep, with her head on his shoulder, before the other Bob-Whites got in. *I'm so glad Nick's father is innocent,* she thought as she drifted off.

New Friends • 18

THE NEXT MORNING dawned bright and clear, taking care of the last worry that had lingered in everyone's mind: that rain might force the bike-athon to be postponed.

The Beldens awakened early, even earlier than usual for a Saturday morning, and this Saturday there was no moaning or groaning to be heard as they got out of bed.

Trixie helped her mother fix a breakfast of waffles and sausage, although, she said, "I don't know if we should eat all day. I want to be plenty hungry when we get to Mr. Maypenny's place this afternoon!"

Mrs. Belden smiled indulgently. "That's a long time from now, dear," she said. "I trust the fresh air and excitement to reawaken the famous Belden appetite."

Trixie laughed. "You're right, as usual, Moms," she said. "I guess we need this big breakfast, after all. And thanks for fixing it for us," she added. "It's really sweet of you, when we're all going to be deserting you on the busiest day of the week around Crabapple Farm."

Mrs. Belden poured heated maple syrup from a pan into a cream pitcher as she replied, "This is a good Saturday for you to take off, Trixie. Next weekend is spring planting time, and after that we'll really get busy around here."

"We'll make it up to you," Trixie said, giving her mother an excited hug as she thought about the drawing of Crabapple Farm that was hidden in her room, ready to present to her mother the next day, which was Mother's Day.

The breakfast was delicious, but Mart, Trixie, and Brian were too excited to linger over it. Long before the station wagon came up the drive, all three were waiting, their jackets on, looking out the front window impatiently.

"They're here!" Trixie called, rushing out the door and climbing into the station wagon, where Honey, Jim, Di, and Dan already waited. Brian and Mart were right behind her, their usual older-brother pose of maturity abandoned.

The Bob-Whites took turns getting out of the car to put up the arrows. At one point, Trixie took a piece of poster board with her and ran ahead to the next point, trying to work off her nervous energy.

By the time the last arrow was up, it was time for everyone to go to their assigned rest stops to wait for the cyclists.

The abandoned house looked totally unmysterious once again as the station wagon pulled into the driveway. *No one would ever believe that, until last night, this house hid a ring of counterfeiters,* Trixie thought. She shuddered as she remembered how close she'd almost come to tragedy the night before. For a moment, she wondered if she should have taken Brian's suggestion and traded assignments with Di or Honey so that she wouldn't have to spend any more time at the house.

Soon, however, the clearing was filled with happy, noisy cyclists, and Trixie had no more time to think about her brush with danger. She checked off each cyclist's name and helped Jim and Brian serve punch and sweet rolls, which Tom Delanoy had dropped off earlier.

Then it was time to load everything into the station wagon and drive to Mr. Maypenny's.

"Can't we follow the bike route over there?" Trixie begged. "I want to see how many cyclists are still riding."

"There's enough traffic on the highway as it is, Trixie," Jim said. "Even with the police escort the cyclists have, I don't feel that we should add to it. We'll have to go back along Glen Road the other way and wait for the bikeathon to get to Mr. Maypenny's."

Wait, wait, wait, Trixie thought. *That's all I ever do. At least today I'm waiting for something pleasant, instead of waiting to be loaded into a van and—and disposed of.* She shivered.

The something that Trixie was waiting for turned out to be very pleasant indeed. All but two of the cyclists had made it to Mr. Maypenny's. The other two had had bike trouble.

"I took them home," Tom Delanoy told the Bob-Whites. "I know all about cars, but those ten-speed bikes are a mystery to me. I couldn't fix them."

Trixie thought about how disappointed the two cyclists must be. Still, they'd both made it past Mrs. Vanderpoel's, which meant they'd earned quite a bit of money for the art department. *And nobody had to drop out because of injury,* she added to herself. *That's wonderful!*

Most of the cyclists clustered excitedly around Mr. Maypenny, who stirred the batch of hunter's stew, tasting it every now and then. Mr. Maypenny's gaunt, weather-beaten face fairly glowed from the heat of the steam rising from the kettle and from all the attention he was getting from the young people.

"Isn't he adorable?" Honey said to Trixie in a low voice.

Trixie nodded. "You know he must have gotten up at dawn to get the fire going and start chopping all the vegetables for the stew. I'd be positively growly by now, but he's having the time of his life!"

Nick Roberts stood apart from the group. He had a large sketch pad and a charcoal pencil, and he was making quick, bold sketches of various scenes from the picnic, which he gave out to the cyclists as souvenirs.

Ben Riker stood close to Nick, watching the young artist sketch. "I'd give anything to be able to draw like that," Ben told Nick after he'd watched him at work for a while.

Nick darted a quick glance at Ben to see if he was being taunted.

"I really mean it," Ben added hastily. "I've always enjoyed sketching—oh, nothing good like these things of yours, you understand. I just do little doodles on my notebook covers or on the message pad by the phone. I was always too afraid that I'd be teased if I took it seriously, so I've never really worked at it. Watching you draw, I really wish I had."

"You're never too old to learn," Nick said, turning the sketch pad to a fresh page and handing the pad and pencil to Ben. "Try drawing that group of people over there." He pointed to two boys and a girl who were chattering happily over their bowls of stew.

Ben's usual composure vanished, and he looked flustered, but he took the pad and pencil and began to draw. Nick looked on critically, giving Ben an occasional bit of advice. When the sketch was finished, Nick studied it for a long time, while Ben looked on anxiously.

"I'd say you have some talent," Nick said. "You should think about taking an art class next year if you're still at Sleepyside. Mr. Crider is a good teacher, and, for a change, there should be no shortage of supplies, now that Trixie and her friends have raised all this money."

The school principal, who had just arrived at the picnic, overheard Nick's comment. "That's right," he agreed. "Actually, that's only the half of it. This bikeathon—and the need for it—has caused a lot of comment in the community. The school board is on the spot for neglecting the art department. Chances are they'll allot a good deal more to the art department budget next year."

Nick, in his excitement at what the principal had just said, pounded Ben Riker on the back. "Did you hear that?" he demanded. "If I work hard enough next year, I can put together a portfolio that will be accepted by any art school in the country. Now that I'm sure of that, I just know I'll be able to scrape together the tuition somehow."

Ben looked enviously at Nick, admiring him for having a dedication that he himself had never felt. "I'm sure you will, Nick. I'm sure you will."

While Nick was getting encouragement from Ben Riker and the principal, Trixie was getting discouragement from Sergeant Molinson, in the form of another stern warning against meddling in police business.

"I told you when you turned in the deutsche mark," he said, "that the counterfeiters would be desperate criminals. Did you listen to me? No! You went out, in the dead of night, without telling anyone where you were going, and got yourself caught by those very same men."

"But—" Trixie started to protest.

"But nothing, Trixie," the sergeant cut her off. "As a policeman for the town of Sleepyside-on-the-Hudson, I'm charged with protecting the safety and well-being of the town's citizens. That includes you, Trixie Belden. Would you tell me, please, how I can do my duty when you insist on taking foolish and unnecessary risks?"

Trixie stared at the ground. She had started to tell the sergeant that she hadn't intended to get herself into a dangerous situation, that she'd simply gone to the abandoned house without thinking to tell anyone. She realized that that excuse would hardly make Sergeant Molinson feel better.

I thought I'd escaped his lecture when he left the abandoned house last night, Trixie thought. *I guess he just went home to rehearse it.* Trixie bit her lower lip. *What an awful thing to think! Sergeant Molinson is just concerned about me. I should be grateful, instead of angry.*

"Anyway," Sergeant Molinson said, apparently feeling that he'd given Trixie enough of a lecture, especially on such a happy day, "you got out of danger unharmed one more time. The two culprits we arrested last night gave us the name of the engraver they got to work for them. And you'll be happy to know that I received a call this morning from the president of a bank in upstate New York. His bank had taken in quite a bit of the counterfeit German currency that ring turned out when they were operating up there. The bank pledged a large sum as a reward to the first person who located the counterfeiters' operation, and some of the other banks in the area added money of their own to the reward.

"It's quite a lot of money all together—about five thousand dollars. That money will go to you, since you discovered the hideout. I suppose that you have a worthy charity all picked out. No?" he questioned, seeing Trixie shaking her head.

"I can't give that money to my favorite charity because I didn't earn it," Trixie said excitedly. "Nick did! He was already hiding in the van when I got to the abandoned house, so that means that he was the first to find it! Wait till I tell him!"

"You don't have to," Nick said over Trixie's shoulder. "I—I couldn't help but overhear." Nick's eyes were shining. "It looks like my problems are all solved, along with the mystery."

Nick looked down at the piece of paper he'd torn out of the sketch pad and was now holding in his hands. "I—I actually came over to give you this, Trixie. It was supposed to be a joke, but now— I'm not sure it's appropriate, but take it anyway."

Nick held out the piece of paper, and Trixie took it. She began to laugh. The other Bob-Whites gathered around her and looked at it, and then they began to laugh, too.

"How can you say this isn't appropriate?" Mart asked. "Why, I can't think of a *more* appropriate pose in which to draw Trixie Belden."

The sketch Nick had drawn was one of Trixie, biting her lower lip and looking contrite, and Sergeant Molinson, towering over her and looking stern.

"It's perfectly perfect!" Honey said. "You haven't known any of us for very long, Nick, but when you have, you'll know that that's a pose that Trixie seems to find herself in fairly often."

"Too often," Trixie admitted. "I'm going to hang this picture in my room and stare at it for thirty minutes every day, to remind myself of what happens when I don't listen to Sergeant Molinson's advice."

"I'm glad you can find a use for this sketch," Nick said. "Someday, though, I'd like to do a really nice drawing of you. I owe you a piece of artwork, remember? After all, I tore one of your posters up."

"I remember," Trixie said. "I understand, now, why you did it. You were upset because you couldn't disobey your father and feeling guilty because you couldn't explain to me why you wouldn't help at the bikeathon. When you saw that poster, your feelings just boiled over—the way mine often do. You don't owe me a portrait because of that, though, Nick."

"Well, if Trixie doesn't want it, I do," Jim said. "I plan to hold you to your promise of drawing a really nice portrait of her, Nick."

While the laughter and conversation bubbled around them, Trixie and Honey walked over to the Bob-Whites' bicycles, which Tom Delanoy had brought over earlier that afternoon. The Bob-Whites had decided that they would lead the way on the last leg of the bikeathon, back to Sleepyside and the end of the route. Soon it would be time to go.

"It all worked out so well, Trixie," Honey said. "We raised a lot of money for the art department, caught the counterfeiters, and made a new friend in the process."

"We made *two* new friends, Honey," Trixie reminded her, looking toward the spot where Ben Riker stood, talking with a group of cyclists. "Things couldn't have worked out better."

"They certainly couldn't have," Dan Mangan said as he, along with the other Bob-Whites, joined the two girls.

"We'd better get everybody back on the road," Brian said, waving his arm to signal the other cyclists. "I'm ready to get home for a rest. It's been a long day."

"We have the whole long, lazy summer coming up in which to rest," Di said luxuriously.

"The only way to achieve that dream," Mart said, "would be to buy back your introduction to

Trixie. You know she's bound to get us into more scrapes before fall rolls around."

"I, for one, am willing to take that risk," Jim said teasingly. "I have a feeling that the rest of you are, too. Come on, Bob-Whites! Let's go!"